Edgar Allan Poe
Analyzes Handwriting:

A Chapter On Autography

by

Edgar Allan Poe

With an Introduction and a
Biographical Dictionary of Poe's Subjects

by

Jim Chevallier

Published by *Chez Jim Books*

The best way to contact the publisher is through e-mail: **jimchev@chezjim.com**.
You may also visit **www.chezjim.com** for the most current contact information.

ISBN: 978-0-6151-8263-6

TABLE OF CONTENTS

INTRODUCTION _____ *v*
    Poe as graphologist _____ v
    Poe as literary observer _____ vii

A Chapter On Autography _____ *1*

CHARLES ANTHON _____ 4

WASHINGTON IRVING _____ 5

PARK BENJAMIN _____ 5

JOHN P. KENNEDY _____ 6

GRENVILLE MELLEN _____ 7

JAMES KIRKE PAULDING _____ 7

LYDIA SIGOURNEY _____ 7

ROBERT WALSH _____ 8

JOSEPH HOLT INGRAHAM _____ 8

WILLIAM CULLEN BRYANT _____ 8

FITZ-GREENE HALLECK _____ 9

NATHANIEL WILLIS _____ 9

RUFUS DAWES _____ 9

HENRY WADSWORTH LONGFELLOW _____ 10

REV. JOHN PIERPONT _____ 10

W. GILMORE SIMMS _____ 11

ORESTES A. BROWNSON _____ 11

JUDGE BEVERLY TUCKER _____ 12

JOHN SANDERSON _____ 12

HANNAH FLAGG GOULD _____ 13

CALEB SPRAGUE HENRY _____ 13

EMMA EMBURY _____ 13

ELIZA LESLIE _____ 13

JOSEPH O'NEAL _____ 14

SEBA SMITH _____ 14

ALEXANDER SLIDELL _____ 15

FRANCIS LIEBER _____ 15

SARAH J. HALE _____ 16

EDWARD EVERETT _____ 16

ROBERT BIRD _____ 16

JOHN NEAL _____ 16

CATHERINE MARIA SEDGWICK _____ 17

JAMES FENIMORE COOPER _____ 17

FRANCIS LISTER HAWKS _____ 17

HENRY WILLIAM HERBERT _____ 17

JOHN GORHAM PALFREY _____ 18

FREDERIC W. THOMAS _____ 18

ROBERT MORRIS _____ 19

EZRA HOLDEN _____ 19

GEORGE REX GRAHAM _____ 19

WILLIAM LEETE STONE _____ 20

JARED SPARKS _____ 20

HUGH SWINTON LEGARE _____ 21

GEORGE LUNT _____ 21

JOSEPH RIPLEY CHANDLER _____ 21

HENRY T. TUCKERMAN _____ 22

LOUIS ANTOINE GODEY _____ 22

JOHN STEPHANSON DU SOLLE _____ 22

JAMES S. FRENCH _____ 23

THEODORE SEDGWICK FAY _____ 23

JOHN KEARSLEY MITCHELL _____ 23

GEORGE P. MORRIS _____ 24

GEORGE HENRY CALVERT _____ 24

JOHN NELSON MCJILTON _____ 24

WILLIAM DAVIS GALLAGHER _____ 25

RICHARD H. DANA _____ 25

MORTON MCMICHAEL _____ 25

NATHAN COVINGTON BROOKS _____ 26

THOMAS H. STOCKTON _____ 26

CHARLES WEST THOMSON _____ 26

WILLIAM ELLERY CHANNING _____ 27

LAMBERT A. WILMER _____ 27

JESSE ERSKINE DOW _____ 28

HORATIO HASTINGS WILD _____ 28

MARGUERITE ST. LEON LOUD _____ 28

PLINY EARLE _____ 29

DAVID HOFFMAN _____ 29

SAMUEL D. LANGTREE _____ 29

ROBERT TAYLOR CONRAD _____ 29

JOHN QUINCY ADAMS _____ 30

PHILIP PENDLETON COOKE _____ 30

JOHN BEAUCHAMP JONES _____ 30

WILLIAM EVANS BURTON _____ 31

RICHARD HENRY WILDE _____ 31

LEWIS CASS _____ 31

JAMES BROOKS _____ 32

JACK DOWNING _____ 32

JAMES RUSSELL LOWELL _____ 32

LEWIS JACOB CIST_____ 33

TIMOTH SHAY ARTHUR _____ 33

JAMES E. HEATH _____ 33

THOMAS HOLLEY CHIVERS_____ 34

JOSEPH STORY _____ 34

JOHN FROST _____ 34

JAMES FREDERICK OTIS _____ 35

JEREMIAH N. REYNOLDS_____ 35

DAVID PAUL BROWN _____ 35

ELIZABETH. CLEMENTINE STEDMAN _____ 36

JOHN GREENLEAF WHITTIER _____ 36

ANN S. STEPHENS_____ 36

APPENDIX _____ 37

CHARLES SPRAGUE _____ 38

CORNELIUS MATHEWS _____ 39

CHARLES FENNO HOFFMAN _____ 39

HORACE GREELEY_____ 39

PROSPER M. WETMORE _____ 40

HENRY WARE_____ 40

WILLIAM E. O. PEABODY _____ 40

EPES SARGENT _____ 41

WASHINGTON ALLSTON _____ 41

ALFRED B. STREET _____ 41

RICHARD PENN SMITH _____ 42

OLIVER WENDEL HOLMES _____ 43

GEORGE WASHINGTON DOANW _____ 43

ALBERT PIKE _____ 43

JAMES MCHENRY _____ 44

REBECCA SHEPHERD REED NICHOLS _____ 44

RICHARD ADAMS LOCKE _____ 44

RALPH WALDO EMERSON _____ 45

A Biographical Dictionary of Poe's Subjects _____ *I*

SOURCES _____ *XIII*

INTRODUCTION

Poe's own introduction tells how he came to write these pieces, which appeared in *Graham's Magazine* starting in 1841 (though he neglects to mention that he also wrote the earlier pieces by "Joseph Miller"). In it, he also neatly resumes their purpose:

> Our design is threefold:—In the first place, seriously to illustrate our position that the mental features are indicated (with certain exceptions) by the handwriting; secondly, to indulge in a little literary gossip; and, thirdly, to furnish our readers with a more accurate and at the same time a more general collection of the autographs of our *literati* than is to be found elsewhere.

My own purpose here is simply to offer some guideposts to the two very different groups who are likely to be the major readers of this work: graphologists and students of Poe and/or the literature of his period. Clearly, these groups may overlap, but it seems most useful to address the different sides of this work separately: that is, as a work of handwriting analysis and as a work of literary criticism.

Poe as graphologist

Modern works on graphology often mention Poe's "Chapter On Autography" as an early classic in the field. This should not mislead readers into thinking that Poe was a handwriting analyst in any modern sense. If he refers to modern elements of graphology – slant, strokes, endings, zones, etc. – it is in a haphazard way. It seems unlikely in fact that he is applying any systematic approach. Numerous biographies mention his interest in cryptography. The same biographies only mention 'autography' – his word for handwriting analysis – in relation to this work and its predecessor.

Much of Poe's analysis assumes a one-to-one relationship between characteristics in the handwriting and characteristics in the person – or, since Poe is sliding in literary critique under the guise of handwriting analysis – the characteristics of the writing: "Judge Tucker's MS. is diminutive, but neat and legible, and has much force and precision, with little of the picturesque. The care which he bestows upon his literary compositions makes itself manifest also in his chirography." – "There is much of the picturesque both in her chirography and in her literary style."

His most dismissive evaluation is of handwriting as a "clerk's" hand: "It is one of the most commonplace clerk's hands which we ever encountered" – "It is an ordinary clerk's hand—one which is met with more frequently than any other" – "somewhat too much in consonance with the ordinary clerk style". This seems to refer to the same uninflected style which a modern graphologist might call a "schoolbook" style, except that Poe – the very personification of individuality – invests it with a dismissive contempt: "His chirography indicates the 'commonplace' upon which we have commented. It is a very usual, scratchy, and tapering clerk's hand—a hand which no man of talent ever did or could indite." He does refer to a "school-boyish" style – "the whole chirography has a constrained and school-boyish air" – but this is even more dismissive than his reference to a 'clerk's' hand.

When Poe does refer to characteristics such as stroke, weight or angularity, he does not seem to be giving them any systematic or emblematic meaning: "A painter called upon to designate the main peculiarity of this MS. would speak at once of the *picturesque*. This character is given it by the absence of hair-strokes, and by the abrupt termination of every letter without tapering; also in great measure by varying the size and slope of the letters." – "Among its regular up and down strokes, waving lines and hair-lines, systematic taperings and flourishes, we look in vain for the force, polish and decision of the poet." – "The hair-strokes differ little from the downward ones, and the MSS. have thus a uniformity they might not otherwise have." – "It has too much tapering, and too much variation between the weight of the hair strokes and the downward ones, to be forcible or picturesque." – "His MS. is a simple unornamented hand, rather rotund than angular, very legible, forcible." He also refers to the difference between some signatures and the rest of the subject's writing but without giving this difference any specific meaning.

He is slightly more modern when he notes how different occupations affect handwriting: "The lawyer, who, pressed for time, is often forced to embody a world of heterogeneous memoranda on scraps of paper, with the stumps of all varieties of pen, will soon find the fair characters of his boyhood degenerate into hieroglyphics which would puzzle Doctor Wallis or Champollion; and from chirography so disturbed it is nearly impossible to decide anything. In a similar manner, men who pass through many striking vicissitudes of life, acquire in each change of circumstance a temporary inflection of the handwriting; the whole resulting, after many years in an unformed or variable MS. scarcely to be recognised by themselves from one day to the other." A modern graphologist might not agree however that "it is nearly impossible to decide anything" from such highly individual writing.

Other examples can be found in this work of references that touch on modern graphological elements without analyzing them from the same perspective. But these brief remarks should give readers some idea of what to expect – and what not – from a graphological point of view.

Finally, Joseph Evans Snodgrass' remark about Poe's "innocent belief of the science of autography" bears repeating: "His own MS., being exceedingly neat and unvaried, refutes his theory – for a more eccentric genius cannot be found..." (the *Saturday Visitor*, November 11, 1841).

Poe as literary observer

The literary interest of this work lies in two points: Poe's comments on other writers and the overview it gives of writers of the period.

Even at the time, it was not lost on some that Poe's remarks on handwriting in this work generally were secondary to his evaluations of each writer. Though, at thirty-two, he had less than ten years to live, he was still a young writer and critic and some of the figures he chose to "analyze" were prominent or at least influential. One critic called his critiques "a colossal piece of impertinence". His remarks here seem to have made him some enemies – to whom he responds defiantly in his introduction to the Appendix: "the voice of him who maintains fearlessly what he believes honestly, is pretty sure to find an echo (if the speaking be not mad) in the vast heart of the world at large."

It is not unusual for young, upcoming writers to be critical of the successful writers of a previous generation. Poe's remarks on several established writers of his time might be viewed in that light. On John Greenleaf Whittier: "especially in *imagination,* ... he is ever remarkably deficient. His themes are *never* to our liking." On William Cullen Bryant: "we look in vain for the force, polish and decision of the poet." On Emerson: "Mr. RALPH WALDO EMERSON belongs to a. class of gentlemen with whom we have no patience whatever—the mystics for mysticism's sake." His remarks on other major figures are often at best qualified.

Beyond such tempting targets, however, we get hints of Poe's literary values in his critiques of lesser-known writers: "Freedom, dignity, precision, and grace, without originality, may be properly attributed to her. She has fine taste, without genius." – "It is an exquisite specimen of mannerism, without meaning and without merit—of an artificial, but most inartistical style of composition, of which conventionality is the soul,—taste, nature, and reason the antipodes. A man may be a clever financier without being a genius." – "In style he is perhaps the most inflated, involved, and falsely-figurative of any of our more noted poets." – "He is often witty, often cuttingly sarcastic, but seldom humorous." – "The extreme of burlesque runs throughout the work, which is also chargeable with a tedious repetition of slang and incident." – "His compositions... are characterized by sweetness rather than strength of versification, and by tenderness and delicacy rather than by vigour or originality of thought." – "the poet's flighty, hyper-fanciful character, with his unsettled and often erroneous ideas of the beautiful" – "It is an exquisite specimen of mannerism, without meaning and without merit—of an artificial, but most inartistical style of composition, of which conventionality is the soul." – "Style regards, more than anything else, the *tone* of a composition. All the rest is not unimportant, to be sure, but appertains to the minor morals of literature, and can be learned by rote by the meanest simpletons in letters—can be carried to its highest excellence by dolts, who, upon the whole, are despicable as stylists." Can a reader of Poe *not* think of "The Bells" in reading "Even his worst nonsense... has an indefinite charm of sentiment and melody. We can never be sure that there is *any* meaning in his words—neither is there any meaning in many of our finest musical airs—but the effect is very similar in both."?

A far longer essay could explore how these and other comments are reflected - or not – in Poe's own work (or even his life: "he has reaped the usual fruits of a spirit of independence, and thus failed to make that impression on the *popular* mind which his talents, under other circumstances, would have effected"). For the present purpose, it is enough to note that "A Chapter On Autography" offers a wealth of such remarks for consideration.

Whatever his estimate of their merit, the mere fact that Poe has decided to include the writers mentioned here is significant. While not all were as important as he suggests, the great majority had sufficient prestige at the time to now interest students of nineteenth century American literature. The very obscurity of others suggests they appear here because of their connection with Poe. While the work is not a complete survey of the American literature of its time, it offers a wide-ranging view of that literature in a very brief space. The biographical dictionary at the end of this volume is intended to help the reader make best use of this information, and to prompt further research on those the reader finds intriguing.

NOTE: *The version of a "A Chapter On Autography" reproduced here is taken from Volume IV of The Works of Edgar Allan Poe, edited by John H. Ingram and published by A&C Black, Ltd. in London in or after 1899. Rather than reproduce this version in facsimile, I have tried to preserve its look and quirks while fitting it more efficiently to the present modern format. These peculiarities include the period that appears after "Autography" in the header, a space after most initial quotation marks, varying quality of graphics, old-fashioned spelling, and the spelling of Oliver Wendell Holmes' middle name with one 'l'. Hopefully these touches, disconcerting as they may be to a modern reader, provide a near, if not exact, sense of what it is like to read the period version of the text.*

A CHAPTER

ON

AUTOGRAPHY

BY

Edgar A Poe

Under this head, some years ago, there appeared in the " Southern Literary Messenger" an article which attracted very general attention, not less from the nature of its subject than from the peculiar manner in which it was handled. The editor introduces his readers to a certain Mr. Joseph Miller, who, it is hinted is not merely a descendant of the illustrious Joe of jest-book notoriety, but is that identical individual in proper person. Upon this point, however, an air of uncertainty is thrown by means of an equivoque, maintained throughout the paper, in respect to Mr. Miller's middle name. This equivoque is put into the mouth of Mr. M. himself. He gives his name, in the first instance, as Joseph A. Miller, but in the course of conversation shifts it to Joseph B., then to Joseph C., and so on through the whole alphabet, until he concludes by desiring a copy of the Magazine to be sent to his address as Joseph Z. Miller, Esquire.

The object of his visit to the editor is to place in his hands the autographs of certain distinguished American *literati*. To these persons he had written rigmarole letters on various topics, and in all cases had been successful in eliciting a reply. The replies only (which it is scarcely necessary to say are all fictitious) are given in the Magazine with a genuine autograph facsimile appended, and are either burlesques of the supposed writer's usual style, or rendered otherwise absurd by reference to the nonsensical questions imagined to have been propounded by Mr. Miller. The autographs thus given are twenty-six in all—corresponding to the twenty-six variations in the initial letter of the hoaxer's middle name.

With the public this article took amazingly well, and many of our principal papers were at the expense of reprinting it with the woodcut autographs. Even those whose names had been introduced, and whose style had been burlesqued, took the joke, generally speaking, in good part. Some of them were at a loss what to make of the matter. Dr. W. E. Channing of Boston was at some trouble, it is said, in calling to mind whether he had or had not actually written to some Mr. Joseph Miller the letter attributed to him in the article. This letter was nothing more than what follows:—

Boston———

Dear Sir—No such person as Philip Philpot has ever been in my employ as a coachman, or otherwise. The name is an odd one, and not likely to be forgotten. The man must have reference to some other Doctor Channing. It would be as well to question him closely.

Respectfully yours,

To Joseph X. Miller, Esq.   W. E. CHANNING.

The precise and brief sententiousness of the divine is here, it will be seen, very truly adopted or " hit off."

In one instance only was the *jeu-d'esprit* taken in serious dudgeon. Colonel Stone and the " Messenger'" had not been upon the best of terms. Some one of the Colonel's little brochures had been severely treated by that journal, which declared that the work would have been far more properly published among the quack advertisements in a spare corner of the " Commercial." The colonel had retaliated by wholesale vituperation of the " Messenger." This being the state of affairs, it was not to be wondered at that the following epistle was not quietly received on the part of him to whom it was attributed:

NEW YORK———

Dear Sir—I am exceedingly and excessively sorry that it is out of my power to comply with your rational and reasonable request. The subject you mention is one with which I am utterly unacquainted. Moreover, it is one about which I know very little.

Respectfully,

Joseph V. Miller. Esq.   W.L. STONE.

These tautologies and anti-climaxes were too much for the colonel, and we are ashamed to say that he committed himself by publishing in the " Commercial" an indignant denial of ever having indited such an epistle.

The principal feature of this autograph article, although perhaps the least interesting, was that of the editorial comment upon the supposed MSS., regarding them as indicative of character. In these comments the design was never more than semi-serious. At times, too, the writer was evidently led into error or injustice through the desire of being pungent—not unfrequently sacrificing truth for the sake of a *bon-mot*. In this manner qualities were often attributed to individuals, which were not so much indicated by their handwriting, as suggested by the spleen of the commentator. But that a strong analogy *does* generally and naturally exist between every man's chirography and character, will be denied by none but the unreflecting. It is not our purpose, however, to enter into the *philosophy* of this subject, either in this portion of the present paper, or in the abstract. What we may have to say will be introduced elsewhere, and in connection with particular MSS. The practical application of the theory will thus go hand in hand with the theory itself:

Our design is threefold:—In the first place, seriously to illustrate our position that the mental features are indicated (with certain exceptions) by the handwriting; secondly, to indulge in a little literary gossip; and, thirdly, to furnish our readers with a more accurate and at the same time a more general collection of the autographs of our *literati* than is to be found elsewhere. Of the first portion of this design we have already spoken. The second speaks for itself. Of the third it is only necessary to say that we are confident of its interest for all lovers of literature. Next to the person of a distinguished man-of-letters, we desire to see his portrait—next to his portrait his autograph. In the latter, especially, there is something which seems to bring him before us in his true idiosyncrasy—in his character of *scribe*. The feeling which prompts to the collection of autographs is a natural and rational one. But complete, or even extensive collections, are beyond the reach of those who themselves do not dabble in the waters of literature. The writer of this article has had opportunities in this way enjoyed by few. The MSS. now lying before him are a motley mass indeed. Here are letters, or other compositions, from every individual in America who has the slightest pretension to literary celebrity. From these we propose to select the most eminent names—as to give *all* would be a work of supererogation. Unquestionably, among those whose claims we are forced to postpone, are several whose high *merit* might justly demand a different treatment; but the rule applicable in a case like this seems to be that of celebrity rather than that of true worth. It will be understood that, in the necessity of selection which circumstances impose upon us, we confine ourselves *to the most noted among the living literati of the country*. The article above alluded to embraced, as we have already stated, only twenty-six names, and was not occupied *exclusively* either with living persons, or properly speaking, with literary ones. In fact the whole paper seemed to acknowledge no law beyond that of whim. Our present essay will be found to include *one hundred autographs*. We have thought it unnecessary to preserve any particular order in their arrangement.

Professor CHARLES ANTHON of Columbia College, New York, is well known
as the most erudite of our classical scholars; and, although still a young man, there
are few, if any, even in Europe, who surpass him in his peculiar path of knowledge.
In England his supremacy has been tacitly acknowledged by the immediate
republication of his editions of Cæsar, Sallust, and Cicero, with other works, and
their adoption as text-books at Oxford and Cambridge. His amplification of
Lemprière did him high honour, but of late has been entirely superseded by a
Classical Dictionary of his own—a work most remarkable for the extent and
comprehensiveness of its details, as well as for its historical, chronological,
mythological, and philological *accuracy*. It has at once completely overshadowed
everything of its kind. It follows, as a matter of course, that Mr. Anthon has many
little enemies among the inditers of merely big books. He has not been unassailed,
yet has assuredly remained uninjured in the estimation of all those whose opinion he
would be likely to value. We do not mean to say that he is altogether without faults,
but a certain antique Johnsonism of style is perhaps one of his worst. He was mainly
instrumental (with Professor Henry and Dr. Hawks) in setting on foot the " New
York Review," a journal of which he is the most efficient literary support, and
whose most erudite papers have always been furnished by his pen.

The chirography of Professor Anthon is the most regularly beautiful of any in
our collection. We see the most scrupulous precision, finish, and neatness about
every portion of it—in the formation of' individual letters, as well as in the *tout-
ensemble*. The perfect symmetry of the MS. gives it, to a casual glance, the appearance
of Italic print. The lines are quite straight, and at exactly equal distances, yet are
written without black rules, or other artificial aid. There is not the slightest
superfluity in the way of flourish or otherwise, with the exception of the twirl in the
C of the signature. Yet the whole is rather neat and graceful than forcible. Of four
letters now lying before us, one is written on pink, one on a faint blue, one on green,
and one on yellow paper—all of the finest quality. The seal is of green wax, with an
impression of the head of Cæsar.

It is in the chirography of such men as Professor Anthon that we look with
certainty for indication of character. The life of a scholar is mostly undisturbed by
those adventitious events which distort the natural disposition of the man of the
world, preventing his real nature from manifesting itself in his MS. The lawyer, who,
pressed for time, is often forced to embody a world of heterogeneous memoranda
on scraps of paper, with the stumps of all varieties of pen, will soon find the fair
characters of his boyhood degenerate into hieroglyphics which would puzzle Doctor
Wallis or Champollion; and from chirography so disturbed it is nearly impossible to
decide anything. In a similar manner, men who pass through many striking
vicissitudes of life, acquire in each change of circumstance a temporary inflection of

the handwriting; the whole resulting, after many years in an unformed or variable MS. scarcely to be recognised by themselves from one day to the other. In the case of literary men generally, we may expect some decisive token of the mental influence upon the MS., and in the instance of the classical devotee we may look with *especial* certainty for such token. We see, accordingly, in Professor Anthon's autography each and all of the known idiosyncrasies of his taste and intellect. We recognise at once the scrupulous precision and finish of his scholarship and of his style—the love of elegance which prompts him to surround himself in his private study with gems of sculptural art and beautifully bound volumes, all arranged with elaborate attention to form, and in the very pedantry of neatness. We perceive, too, the disdain of superfluous embellishment which distinguishes his compilations, and which gives to their exterior appearance so marked an air of Quakerism. We must not forget to observe that the " want of force" is a want as perceptible in the whole character of the man as in that of the MS.

The MS. of Mr. IRVING has little about it indicative of his genius. Certainly, no one could suspect from it any nice *finish* in the writer's compositions; nor is this nice finish to be found. The letters now before us vary remarkably in appearance; and those of late date are not nearly so well written as the more antique. Mr. Irving has travelled much, has seen many vicissitudes, and has been so thoroughly satiated with fame as to grow slovenly in the performance of his literary tasks. This slovenliness has affected his handwriting. But even from his earlier MSS. there is little to be gleaned, except the ideas of simplicity and precision. It must be admitted, however, that this fact, in itself, is characteristic of the literary manner, which, however excellent, has no prominent or very remarkable features.

For the last six or seven years few men have occupied a more desirable position among us than Mr. BENJAMIN. As the editor of the " American Monthly Magazine," of the " New Yorker," and more lately of the " Signal," and " New World," he has exerted an influence scarcely second to that of any editor in the country. This influence Mr., B. owes to no single cause, but to his combined ability, activity, causticity, fearlessness, and independence. We use the latter term, however, with some mental reservation. The editor of the " World" is independent so far as the word implies unshaken resolution to follow the bent of one's own will, let the consequences be what they may. He is no respecter of persons, and his vituperation as often assails the powerful as the powerless—indeed the latter fall rarely under his censure. But we cannot call his independence at all times that of principle. We can never be sure that he will defend a cause merely because it is the cause of truth—or even because he regards it as such. He is too frequently biassed by personal feelings—feelings now of friendship, and again of vindictiveness. He is a warm friend, and a bitter, but not implacable enemy. His judgment in literary matters should not be questioned, but there is some difficulty in getting at his real opinion. As a prose writer, his style is lucid, terse, and pungent. He is often witty, often cuttingly sarcastic, but seldom humorous. He frequently injures the force of his fiercest attacks by an indulgence in merely vituperative epithets. As a poet, he is entitled to far higher consideration than that in which he is ordinarily held. He is skilful and passionate, as well as imaginative. His sonnets have not been surpassed. In short, it is as a poet that his better genius is evinced—it is in poetry that his noble spirit breaks forth, showing what the man is, and what, but for unhappy circumstances, he would invariably appear.

Mr. Benjamin's MS. is not very dissimilar to Mr. Irving's, and, like his, it has no doubt been greatly modified by the excitements of life, and by the necessity of writing much and hastily, so that we can predicate but little respecting it. It speaks of his exquisite sensibility and passion. These betray themselves in the nervous variation of the MS. as the subject is diversified. When the theme is an ordinary one, the writing is legible and has force, but when it verges upon anything which may be supposed to excite, we see the characters falter as they proceed. In the MSS. of some of his best poems this peculiarity is very remarkable. The signature conveys the idea of his *usual* chirography.

Mr. KENNEDY is well known as the author of " Swallow Barn," " Horse-Shoe Robinson," and " Rob of the Bowl," three works whose features are strongly and decidedly marked. These features are boldness and force of thought (disdaining ordinary embellishment, and depending for its effect upon masses rather than upon details), with a predominant *sense of the picturesque* pervading and giving colour to the whole. His " Swallow Barn " in especial (and it is by the first effort of an author that we form the truest idea of his mental bias) is but a rich succession of picturesque still-life pieces. Mr. Kennedy is well-to-do in the world. and has always taken the world easily. We may therefore expect to find in his chirography, if ever in any, a full indication of the chief feature of his literary style, especially as this chief feature is so remarkably prominent. A glance at his signature will convince anyone that the indication is to be found. A painter called upon to designate the main peculiarity of this MS. would speak at once of the *picturesque*. This character is given it by the absence of hair-strokes, and by the abrupt termination of every letter without tapering; also in great measure by varying the size and slope of the letters. Great uniformity is preserved in the whole air of the MS., with great variety in the constituent parts. Every character has the clearness, boldness, and precision of a woodcut. The long letters do not rise or fall in an undue degree above the others. Upon the whole, this is a hand which pleases us much, although its *bizarrerie* is rather too piquant for the general taste. Should its writer devote himself more exclusively to light letters we predict his future eminence. The paper on which our epistles are written is very fine, clear, and *white,* with gilt edges. The seal is neat, and just sufficient wax has been used for the impression. All this betokens a love of the elegant without effeminacy.

The handwriting of GRENVILLE MELLEN is somewhat peculiar, and partakes largely of the character of his signature as seen above. The whole is highly indicative of the poet's flighty, hyper-fanciful character, with his unsettled and often erroneous ideas of the beautiful. His straining after effect is well paralleled in the formation of the preposterous G in the signature, with the two dots by its side. Mr. Mellen has genius unquestionably, but there is something in his temperament which obscures it.

No correct notion of Mr. PAULDING'S literary peculiarities can be obtained from an inspection of his MS., which no doubt has been strongly modified by adventitious circumstances. His small *a*'s, *t*'s, and *c*'s are all alike, and the style of the characters generally is French, although the entire MS. has much the appearance of Greek text. The paper which he ordinarily uses is of a very fine glossy texture, and of a blue tint, with gilt edges. His signature is a good specimen of his general hand.

Mrs. SIGOURNEY seems to take much pains with her MSS. Apparently she employs *black lines.* Every *t* is crossed, and every *i* dotted, with precision, while the punctuation is faultless. Yet the whole has nothing of effeminacy or formality. The individual characters are large, well and freely formed, and preserve a perfect uniformity throughout. Something in her handwriting puts us in mind of Mr. Paulding's. In both MSS. perfect regularity exists, and in both the style is *formed* or *decided.* Both are beautiful, yet Mrs. Sigourney's is the most legible, and Mr. Paulding's nearly the most illegible in the world. From that of Mrs. S. we might easily form a true estimate of her compositions. Freedom, dignity, precision, and grace, without originality, may be properly attributed to her. She has fine taste, without genius. Her paper is usually good, the seal small, of green and gold wax, and without impression.

Robert Walsh

Mr. WALSH'S MS. is peculiar, from its large, sprawling, and irregular appearance—rather rotund than angular. It always seems to have been hurriedly written. The *f*'s are crossed with a sweeping scratch of the pen, which gives to his epistles a somewhat droll appearance. A *dictatorial* air pervades the whole. His paper is of ordinary quality. His seal is commonly of brown wax mingled with gold, and bears a Latin motto, of which only the words *trans* and *mortuus* are legible.

Mr. Walsh cannot be denied talent, but his reputation, which has been bolstered into being by a *clique,* is not a thing to live. A blustering self-conceit betrays itself in his chirography, which upon the whole is not very dissimilar to that of Mr. E. Everett, of whom we shall speak hereafter.

J. H. Ingraham

Mr. INGRAHAM, or lngrahame (for he writes his name sometimes with, and sometimes without the *e),* is one of our most *popular* novelists, if not one of our best. He appeals always to the taste of the ultra-romanticists (as a matter, we believe, rather of pecuniary policy than of choice) and thus is obnoxious to the charge of a. certain cut-and-thrust, blue-fire, melodramaticism. Still, he is capable of better things. His chirography is very unequal, at times sufficiently clear and flowing, at others shockingly scratchy and uncouth. From it nothing whatever can be predicated except an uneasy vacillation of temper and of purpose.

W. C. Bryant

Mr. BRYANT'S MS. puts us entirely at fault. It is one of the most commonplace clerk's hands which we ever encountered, and has no character about it beyond that of the day-book and ledger. He writes, in short, what mercantile men and professional penman call a fair hand, but what artists would term an abominable one. Among its regular up and down strokes, waving lines and hair-lines, systematic taperings and flourishes, we look in vain for the force, polish and decision of the poet. The *picturesque,* to be sure, is equally deficient in his chirography and in his poetical productions.

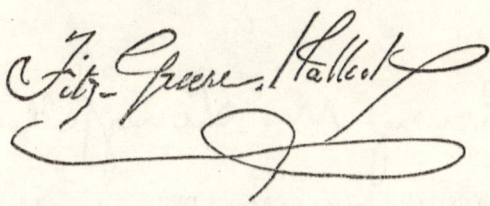

Mr. HALLECK'S hand is strikingly indicative of genius. We see in it some force, more grace, and little of the picturesque. There is a great deal of freedom about it and his MSS. seem to be written *currente calamo*, but without hurry. His flourishes, which are not many, look as if thoughtfully planned, and deliberately, yet firmly executed. His paper is very good, and of a bluish tint, his seal is of red wax.

Mr. WILLIS when writing carefully would write a hand nearly resembling that of Mr. Halleck, although no similarity is perceptible in the signatures. His usual chirography is dashing, free, and not ungraceful, but is sadly deficient in force and picturesqueness. It has been the fate of this gentleman to be alternately condemned *ad infinitum*, and lauded *ad nauseam*, a fact which speaks much in his praise. We know of no American writer who has evinced greater versatility of talent, that is to say, of high talent, often amounting to genius, and we know of none who has more narrowly missed placing himself at the head of our letters.

The paper of Mr. Willis's epistles is always fine and glossy. At present he employs a somewhat large seal, with a dove or carrier-pigeon at the top, the word " Glenmary" at bottom, and the initials " N. P. W." in the middle.

Mr. DAWES has been long known as a poet, but his claims are scarcely yet settled, his friends giving him rank with Bryant and Halleck, while his opponents treat his pretensions with contempt. The truth is that the author of " Geraldine" and " Athenia of Damascus" has written occasional verses very well—so well that some of his minor pieces may be considered equal to any of the minor pieces of either of the two gentlemen above mentioned. His longer poems, however, will not bear examination. " Athenia of Damascus" is pompous nonsense, and " Geraldine" a most ridiculous imitation of Don Juan, in which the beauties of the original have been as sedulously avoided as the blemishes have been blunderingly culled. In style he is perhaps the most inflated, involved, and falsely-figurative of any of our more noted poets. This defect of course is only fully appreciable in what are termed his " sustained efforts," and thus his shorter pieces are often exceedingly good. His apparent erudition is mere verbiage, and were it real would be lamentably out of place where we see it. He seems to have been infected with a blind admiration of Coleridge, especially of his mysticism and cant.

Henry W. Longfellow [signature]

H. W. LONGFELLOW (Professor of Moral Philosophy at Harvard), is entitled to the first place among the poets of America—certainly to the first place among those who have put themselves prominently forth as poets. His good qualities are all of the highest order, while his sins are chiefly those of affectation and imitation-an imitation sometimes verging upon downright theft. His MS. is remarkably good, and is fairly exemplified in the signature. We see here plain indications of the force, vigour, and glowing richness of his literary style; the deliberate and steady *finish* of his compositions. The man who writes thus may not accomplish much, but what he does, will always be thoroughly done. The main beauty or at least one great beauty of his poetry, is that of *proportion;* another is a freedom from extraneous embellishment. He oftener runs into affectation through his endeavours at simplicity, than through any other cause. Now this rigid simplicity and proportion are easily perceptible in the MS., which, altogether, is a very excellent one.

J Pierpont [signature]

The Rev. J. PIERPONT, who, of late, has attracted so much of the public attention, is one of the most accomplished poets in America. His " Airs of Palestine" is distinguished by the sweetness and vigour of its versification, and by the grace of its sentiments. Some of his shorter pieces are exceedingly terse and forcible, and none of our readers can have forgotten his " Lines on Napoleon." His rhythm is at least equal in strength and modulation to that of any poet in America. Here he resembles Milman and Croly.

His chirography, nevertheless, indicates nothing beyond the common place. It is an ordinary clerk's hand—one which is met with more frequently than any other. It is decidedly *formed;* and we have no doubt that he *never* writes otherwise than this. The MS. of his school-days has probably been persisted in to the last. If so, the fact is in full consonance with the steady precision of his style. The flourish at the end of the signature is but a part of the writer's general enthusiasm.

Mr. SIMMS is the author of " Martin Faber," " Atalantis," " Guy Rivers," " The Partisan," " Mellichampe," " The Yemassee," " The Damsel of Darien," " The Black Riders of the Congarce," and one or two other productions, among which we must not forget to mention several fine poems. As a poet, indeed, we like him far better than as a novelist. His qualities in this latter respect *resemble* those of Mr. Kennedy, although he equals him in no particular, except in his appreciation of the graceful. In his sense of beauty he is Mr. K.'s superior, but falls behind him in force, and the other attributes of the author of " Swallow Barn." These differences and resemblances are well shown in the MSS. That of Mr. S. has more slope, and more uniformity in detail, with less in the mass—while it has also less of the picturesque, although still much. The middle name is Gilmore; in the cut it looks like Gilmere.

The REV. ORESTES A. BROWNSON is chiefly known to the literary world as the editor of the " Boston Quarterly Review," a work to which he contributes, each quarter, at least two-thirds of the matter. He has published little in book-form—his principal works being " Charles Elwood" and " New Views." Of these, the former production is, in many respects, one of the highest merit. In logical accuracy, in comprehensiveness of thought, and in the evident frankness and desire for truth in which it is composed, we know of few theological treatises which can be compared with it. Its conclusion, however, bears about it a species of hesitation and inconsequence which betray the fact that the writer has not altogether succeeded in convincing himself of those important truths which he is so anxious to impress upon his readers. We must bear in mind, however, that this is the fault of Mr. Brownson's subject, and not of Mr. Brownson. However well a man may reason on the great topics of God and immortality, he will be forced to admit tacitly in the end, that God and immortality are things to be felt, rather than demonstrated.

On subjects less indefinite, Mr. B. reasons with the calm and convincing force of a Combe. He is, in every respect, an extraordinary man, and with the more extensive resources which would have been afforded him by early education, could not have failed to bring about important results.

His MS. indicates, in the most striking manner, the unpretending simplicity, directness, and especially the *indefatigability* of his mental character. His signature is more *petite* than his general chirography.

JUDGE BEVERLY TUCKER, of the College of William and Mary, Virginia, is the author of one of the best novels ever published in America—" George Balcombe"—although for some reason the book was never a popular favourite. It was, perhaps, somewhat too didactic for the general taste.

He has written a great deal also for the " Southern Literary Messenger" at different times and at one period acted in part, if not altogether, as editor of that Magazine, which is indebted to him for some very racy articles, in the way of criticism especially. He is apt, however, to be led away by personal feelings, and is more given to vituperation for the mere sake of *point* or pungency than is altogether consonant with his character as judge. Some five years ago there appeared in the " Messenger," under. the editorial head, an article on the subject of the " Pickwick Papers" and some other productions of Mr. Dickens. This article, which abounded in well-written but extravagant denunciation of everything composed by the author of " The Curiosity Shop," and which prophesied his immediate downfall, we have reason to believe was from the pen of Judge Beverly Tucker. We take this opportunity of mentioning the subject, because the odium of the paper in question fell altogether upon our shoulders, and it is a burthen we are not disposed and never intended to bear. The review appeared in March, we think, and we had retired from the " Messenger" in the January preceding. About eighteen months previously, and when Mr. Dickens was scarcely known to the public at all, except as the author of some brief tales and essays, the writer of this article took occasion to predict in the " Messenger," and in the most emphatic manner, that high and just distinction which the author in question has attained. Judge Tucker's MS. is diminutive, but neat and legible, and has much force and precision, with little of the picturesque. The care which he bestows upon his literary compositions makes itself manifest also in his chirography. The signature is more florid than the general hand.

Mr. SANDERSON, Professor of the Greek and Latin languages in the High School of Philadelphia, is well known as the author of a series of letters entitled " The American in Paris." These are distinguished by ease and vivacity of style, with occasional profundity of observation, and, above all, by the frequency of their illustrative anecdotes and figures. In all these particulars Professor Sanderson is the precise counterpart of Judge Beverly Tucker, author of " George Balcombe." The MSS. of the two gentlemen are nearly identical. Both are neat, clear, and legible. Mr. Sanderson's is somewhat the more crowded.

H. F. Gould.

About Miss GOULD's MS. there is great neatness, picturesqueness, and finish, without over-effeminacy. The literary style of one who writes thus will always be remarkable for sententiousness and epigramattism; and these are the leading features of Miss Gould's poetry.

C. S. Henry

Prof. HENRY, of Bristol College, is chiefly known by his contributions to our Quarterlies, and as one of the originators of the "New York Review," in conjunction with Dr. Hawks and Professor Anthon. His chirography is neat and picturesque (much resembling that of Judge Tucker), and now excessively scratchy, *clerky*, and slovenly—so that it is nearly impossible to say anything respecting it, except that it indicates a vacillating disposition, with unsettled ideas of the beautiful. None of his epistles, in regard to their chirography, end as well as they begin. This trait denotes *fatigability*. His signature, which is bold and decided, conveys not the faintest idea of the general MS.

Emma C. Embury

Mrs. EMBURY is chiefly known by her contributions to the Periodicals of the country. She is one of the most nervous of our female writers, and is not destitute of originality, that rarest of all qualities in a woman, and especially in an American woman.

Her MS. evinces a strong disposition to fly off at a tangent from the old formulae of the Boarding Academies. Both in it, and in her literary style, it would be well that she should no longer hesitate to discard the absurdities of mere fashion.

Eliza Leslie

Miss LESLIE is celebrated for the homely naturalness of her stories and for the broad satire of her comic style. She has written much for the Magazines. Her chirography is distinguished for neatness and finish, without over-effeminacy. It is rotund, and somewhat diminutive; the letters being separate, and the words always finished with an inward twirl. She is never particular about the quality of her paper or the other externals of epistolary correspondence. From her MSS. in general, we might suppose her solicitous rather about the effect of her compositions as a whole, than about the polishing of the constituent parts. There is much of the picturesque both in her chirography and in her literary style.

Joseph C. Neal [signature]

Mr. NEAL has acquired a very extensive reputation through his " Charcoal Sketches," a series of papers originally written for the " Saturday News" of this city, and afterwards published in book form, with illustrations by Johnston. The whole design of the " Charcoal Sketches" may be stated as the depicting of the wharf and street *loafer;* but this design has been executed altogether in caricature. The extreme of burlesque runs throughout the work, which is also chargeable with a tedious repetition of slang and incident. The loafer always declaims the same nonsense, in the same style, get drunk in the same way, and is taken to the watch-house after the same fashion. Reading one chapter of the book we read all. Any single description would have been an original idea well executed: but the dose is repeated *ad nauseam,* and betrays a worse poverty of' invention. The manner in which Mr. Neal's book was belauded by his personal friends of the Philadelphia press speaks little for their independence, or less for their taste. To dub the author of these " Charcoal Sketches" (which are really very excellent police-reports), with the title of " the American Boz," is either outrageous nonsense or malevolent irony.

In other respects, Mr. N. has evinced talents which cannot be questioned. He has conducted the " Pennsylvanian" with credit, and, as a political writer, he stands deservedly high. His MS. is simple and legible, with much space between the words. It has force, but little grace. Altogether, his chirography is good; but as he belongs to the editorial corps, it would not be just to suppose that any deductions in respect to character could be gleaned from it. His signature conveys the general MS. with accuracy.

Seba Smith [signature]

Mr. SEBA SMITH has become somewhat widely celebrated as the author, in part, of the " Letters of Major Jack Downing". These were very clever productions; coarse, but full of fun, wit, sarcasm, and sense. Their manner rendered them exceedingly popular, until their success tempted into the field a host of brainless imitators. Mr. S. is also the author of several poems; among others, of " Powhatan, a Metrical Romance," which we do not very particularly admire. His MS. is legible, and has much simplicity about it. At times it vacillates, and appears unformed. Upon the whole, it is much such a MS. as David Crockett wrote, and precisely such a one as we might imagine would be written by a *veritable* Jack Downing—by Jack Downing himself, had this creature of Mr. Smith's fancy been endowed with a real entity. The fact is that " The Major" is not a creation; at least one-half of his character actually exists in the bosom of his originator. It was the Jack Downing half that composed " Powhatan."

Alexander Slidell

Lieutenant SLIDELL some years age took the additional name of Mackenzie. His reputation at one period was extravagantly high—a circumstance owing, in some measure, to the *esprit de corps* of the navy, of which he is a member, and to his private influence, through his family, with the Review-cliques. Yet his fame was not altogether undeserved; although it cannot be denied that his first book, " A Year in Spain," was in some danger of being overlooked by his countrymen, until a benignant star directed the attention of the London Bookseller, Murray, to its merits. Cockney octavos prevailed; and the clever young writer, who was cut dead in his Yankee habiliments, met with bows innumerable in the gala dress of an English *imprimatur.* The work now ran through several editions, and prepared the public for the kind reception of " The American in England," which exalted his reputation to its highest pinnacle. Both these books abound in racy description, but are chiefly remarkable for their gross deficiencies in grammatical construction.

Lieut. Slidell's MS. is peculiarly neat and even—quite legible, but altogether too *petite* and effeminate. Few tokens of his literary character are to be found beyond the *petiteness,* which is exactly analogous with the minute detail of his descriptions.

Francis Lieber

FRANCIS LIEBER is Professor of History and Political Economy in the College of South Carolina, and has published many works distinguished by acumen and erudition. Among these we may notice a " Journal of a Residence in Greece," written at the instigation of the historian Niebuhr; " The Stranger in America," a piquant book abounding in various information relative to the United States; a treatise on " Education;" " Reminiscences of an Intercourse with Niebuhr;" and an " Essay on International Copyright"—this last a valuable work. Professor Lieber's personal character is that of the best and most unpretending *bonhommie,* while his erudition is rather massive than minute. We may therefore expect his MS. to differ widely from that of his brother scholar Professor Anthon; and so in truth it does. His chirography is careless, heavy, black, and forcible, without the slightest attempt at ornament-very similar, upon the whole, to the well-known chirography of Chief-Justice Marshall. His letters have the peculiarity of a wide margin left at the top of each page.

[signature: Sarah J. Hale]

    Mrs. HALE is well known for her masculine style of thought. This is clearly expressed in her chirography, which is far larger, heavier, and altogether bolder than that of her sex generally. It resembles in a great degree that of Professor Lieber, and is not easily deciphered.

[signature: Edward Everett]

    Mr. EVERETT's MS. is a noble one. It has about it an air of deliberate precision emblematic of the statesman, and a mingled grace and solidity betokening the scholar. Nothing can be more legible, and nothing need be more uniform. The man who writes thus will never grossly err in judgment or otherwise; but we may also venture to say that he will never attain the loftiest pinnacle of renown. The letters before us have a seal of red wax, with an oval device bearing the initials E.E. and surrounded with a scroll, inscribed with some Latin words which are illegible.

[signature: R. M. Bird]

    Dr. BIRD is well known as the author of " The Gladiator," " Calavar," " The Infidel," " Nick of the Woods," and some other works -" Calavar" being, we think, by far the best of them, and beyond doubt one of the best of American novels. His chirography resembles that of Mr. Benjamin very closely; the chief difference being in a curl of the final letters in Dr. B.'s. The characters, too, have the air of not being able to keep pace with the thought, and an uneasy want of finish seems to have been the consequence. A vivid imagination might easily be deduced from such a MS.

[signature: John Neal]

    Mr. JOHN NEAL'S MS is exceedingly illegible and careless. Many of his epistles are perfect enigmas, and we doubt whether he could read them himself in half-au-hour after they are penned. Sometimes four or five words are run together. Anyone, from Mr. Neal's penmanship, might suppose his mind to be what it really is— excessively flighty and irregular, but active and energetic.

C M Sedgwick

The penmanship of Miss SEDGWICK is excellent. The characters are well-sized, distinct, elegantly but not ostentatiously formed, and, with perfect freedom of manner, are still sufficiently feminine. The hair-strokes differ little from the downward ones, and the MSS. have thus a uniformity they might not otherwise have. The paper she generally uses is good, blue, and machine-ruled. Miss Sedgwick's handwriting points unequivocally to the traits of her literary style—which are strong common sense, and a masculine disdain of mere ornament. The signature conveys the general chirography.

J. Fenimore Cooper

Mr. COOPER'S MS. is very bad—*unformed,* with little of distinctive character about it, and varying greatly in different epistles. In most of those before us a steel pen has been employed, the lines are crooked, and the whole chirography has a constrained and school-boyish air. The paper is fine, and of a bluish tint. A wafer is always used. Without appearing ill-natured, we could scarcely draw any inferences from such a MS. Mr. Cooper bas seen many vicissitudes, and it is probable that, he has not always written thus. Whatever are his faults, his genius cannot be doubted.

F. L. Hawks

Dr. HAWKS is one of the originators of the " New York Review," to which journal he has furnished many articles. He is also known as the author of the " History of the Episcopal Church of Virginia," and one or two minor works. He now edits the " Church Record." His style, both as a writer and as a preacher, is characterised rather by a perfect *fluency* than by any more lofty quality, and this trait is strikingly indicated in his chirography, of which. the signature is a fair specimen.

Henry Wm Herbert

This gentleman is the author of " Cromwell," " The Brothers," " Ringwood, the Rover," and some other minor productions. He at one time edited the " American Monthly Magazine" in connection with Mr. Hoffman. In his compositions for the Magazines, Mr. HERBERT is in the habit of doing both them and himself gross injustice by neglect and hurry. His longer works evince much ability, although he is rarely entitled to be called original. His MS. is exceedingly neat, clear, and forcible; the signature affording a just idea of it. It resembles that of Mr. Kennedy very nearly; but has more slope and uniformity, with, of course, less spirit, and less of the picturesque. He who writes as Mr. Herbert, will be found always to depend chiefly upon his merits of *style* for a literary reputation, and will not be unapt to fall into a pompous grandiloquence. The author of " Cromwell" is sometimes woefully turgid.

Professor PALFREY is known to the public principally through his editorship of the " North American Review." He has a reputation for scholarship; and many of the articles which are attributed to his pen evince that this reputation is well based, so far as the common notion of scholarship extends. For the rest, he seems to dwell altogether within the narrow world of his *own* conceptions; imprisoning them by the very barrier which he has erected against the conceptions of others.

His MS. shows a total deficiency in the sense of the beautiful. It has great pretension—great straining after effect, but is altogether one of the most miserable MSS. in the world—forceless, graceless, tawdry, vacillating and unpicturesque. The signature conveys but a faint idea of its extravagance. However much we may admire the mere *knowledge* of the man who writes thus, it will not do to place any dependence upon his wisdom or upon his taste.

F. W. THOMAS, who began his literary career at the early age of seventeen, by a poetical lampoon upon certain Baltimore fops, has since more particularly distinguished himself as a novelist. His " Clinton Bradshawe" is perhaps better known than any of his later fictions. It is remarkable for a frank, unscrupulous portrait of men and things, in high life and low, and by unusual discrimination and observation in respect to character. Since its publication he has produced " East and West" and " Howard Pinckney," neither of which seems to have been so popular as his first essay, although both have merit.

" East and West," published in 1836, was an attempt to portray the every-day events occurring to a fallen family emigrating from the East to the West. In it, as in " Clinton Bradshawe," most of the characters are drawn from life. " Howard Pinckney" was published in 1840.

Mr. Thomas was at one period the editor of the Cincinnati " Commercial Advertiser." He is also well known as a public lecturer on a variety of topics. His conversational powers are very great. As a poet, he has also distinguished himself. His " Emigrant" will be read with pleasure by every person of taste.

His MS. is more like that of Mr. Benjamin than that of any other literary person of our acquaintance. It has even more than the occasional nervousness of Mr. B.'s, and, as in the case of the editor of the " New World, " indicates the passionate sensibility of the man.

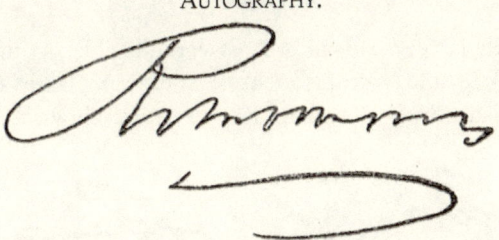

Mr. MORRIS ranks, we believe, as the first of our Philadelphia poets since the death of Willis Gaylord Clark. His compositions, like those of his late lamented friend, are characterised by sweetness rather than strength of versification, and by tenderness and delicacy rather than by vigour or originality of thought. A late notice of him in the " Boston Notion" from the pen of Rufus W. Griswold, did his high qualities no more than justice. As a prose writer, he is chiefly known by his editorial contributions to the Philadelphia " Inquirer," and by occasional essays for the Magazines.

His chirography is usually very illegible, although at times sufficiently distinct. It has no marked characteristics, and like that of almost every editor in the country, has been so modified by the circumstances of his position as to afford no certain indication of the mental features.

EZRA HOLDEN has written much, not only for his paper, " The Saturday Courier," but for our periodicals generally, and stands high in the public estimation, as a sound thinker, and still more particularly as a fearless expresser of his thoughts.

His MS. (which we are constrained to say is a shockingly bad one, and whose general features may be seen in his signature,) indicates the frank and *naïve* manner of his literary style—a style which not unfrequently flies off into whimsicalities.

Mr. GRAHAM is known to the literary world as the editor and protector of " Graham's Magazine," the most popular periodical in America, and also of the " Saturday Evening Post," of Philadelphia. For both of these journals he has written much and well.

His MS. generally is very bad, or at least very illegible. At times it is sufficiently distinct, and has force and picturesqueness, speaking plainly of the *energy* which particularly distinguishes him as a man. The signature above is more scratchy than usual.

Colonel STONE, the editor of the New York " Commercial Advertiser," is remarkable for the great difference which exists between the apparent public opinion respecting his abilities and the real estimation in which he is privately held. Through his paper, and a bustling activity always prone to thrust itself forward, he has attained an unusual degree of influence in New York, and, not only this, but what appears to be a reputation for talent. But this talent we do not remember ever to have heard assigned him by any honest men's private opinion. We place him among our *literati* because he has published certain books. Perhaps the best of these are his " Life of Brandt," and " Life and Times of Red Jacket." Of the rest, his story called" Ups and Downs," his defence of Animal Magnetism, and his pamphlets concerning Maria Monk, are scarcely the most absurd. His MS. is heavy and sprawling, resembling his mental character in a species of utter unmeaningness, which lies like the nightmare, upon his autograph.

The labours of Mr. SPARKS, Professor of History at Harvard, are well known and justly appreciated. His MS. has an unusually odd appearance. The characters are large, round, black, irregular, and perpendicular—the signature, as above, being an excellent specimen of his chirography in general. In all his letters now before us, the lines are as close together as possible, giving the idea of irretrievable confusion; still none of them are illegible upon close inspection. We can form no guess in regard to any mental peculiarities from Mr. Sparks' MSS., which has been no doubt modified by the hurrying and intricate nature of his researches. We might imagine such epistles as these to have been written in extreme haste, by a man exceedingly busy, among great piles of books and papers huddled up around him, like the chaotic tomes of Magliabecihi. The paper used in all our epistles is uncommonly fine.

The name of H. S. LEGARE is written without an accent on the final *e*, yet is pronounced as if this letter were accented,—Legray. He contributed many articles of high merit to the " Southern Review," and has a wide reputation for scholarship and talent. His MS. resembles that of Mr. Palfrey of the " North American Review," and their mental features appear to us nearly identical. What we have said in regard to the chirography of Mr. Palfrey will apply with equal force to that of the present Secretary.

Mr. GEORGE LUNT of Newburyport, Massachusetts, is known as a poet of much vigour of style and massiveness of thought. He delights in the grand, rather than in the beautiful, and is not unfrequently turgid, but never feeble. The traits here described impress themselves with remarkable distinctness upon his chirography, of which the signature gives a perfect idea.

Mr.. CHANDLER'S reputation as the editor of one of the best daily papers in the country, and as one of our finest *belles lettres* scholars, is deservedly high. He is well known through his numerous addresses, essays, miscellaneous sketches, and prose tales. Some of these latter evince imaginative powers of a superior order.

His MS. is not fairly shown in his signature, the latter being much more open and bold than his general chirography. His handwriting must be included in the editorial category—it seems to have been ruined by habitual hurry.

H. T. Tuckerman

H. T. TUCKERMAN has written one or two books consisting of " Sketches of Travel." His " Isabel" is, perhaps, better known than any of his other productions, but was never a popular work He is a *correct* writer so far as mere English is concerned but an insufferably tedious and dull one. He has contributed much of late days to the " Southern Literary Messenger," with which journal, perhaps, the legibility of his MS. has been an important, if not the principal recommendation. His chirography is neat and distinct, and has some grace, but no force—evincing, in a remarkable degree, the idiosyncrasies of the writer.

Mr. GODEY is only known to the literary world as editor and publisher of " The Lady's Book," but his celebrity in this regard entitles him to a place in this collection. His MS. is remarkably distinct and graceful—the signature affording an excellent idea of it. The man who invariably writes so well as Mr. G. invariably does give evidence of a fine taste combined with an indefatigability which will ensure his permanent success in the world's affairs. No man has warmer friends or fewer enemies.

John S. Du Solle

Mr. DU SOLLE is well known through his connection with the " Spirit of the Times." His prose is forcible, and often excellent in other respects. As a poet, he is entitled to higher consideration. Some of his Pindaric pieces are unusually good, and it may be doubted if we have a better *versifier* in America.

Accustomed to the daily toil of an editor, he has contracted a habit of writing hurriedly, and his MS. varies with the occasion. It is impossible to deduce any inferences from it as regards the mental character. The signature shows rather how he can write than how he does.

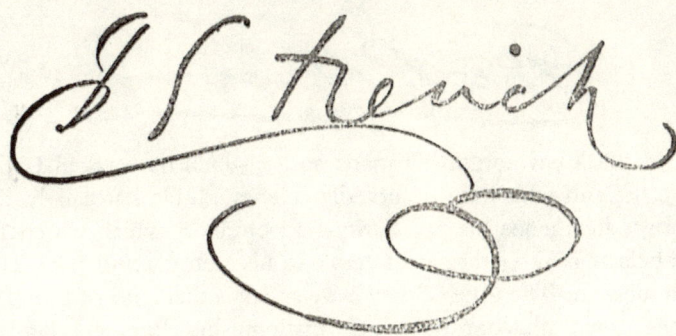

Mr. FRENCH is the author of a " Life of David Crockett" and also of a novel called " Elkswattawa," a denunciatory review of which, in the " Southern Messenger" some years ago, deterred him from further literary attempts should he write again, he will probably distinguish himself, for he is unquestionably a man of talent. We need no better evidence of this than his MS., which speaks of force, boldness, and originality. The flourish, however, betrays a certain *timidity* of taste.

The author of " Norman Leslie" and " The Countess Ida" has been more successful as an essayist about small matters than as a novelist. "Norman Leslie" is more familiarly remembered as "' The Great Used Up," while " The Countess" made no definite impression whatever. Of course we are not to expect remarkable features in Mr. FAY'S MS. It has a wavering, finicky, and over-delicate air, without pretension to either grace or force; and the description of the chirography would answer, without alteration, for that of the literary character. Mr. F. frequently employs an amanuensis, who writes a very beautiful French hand. The one must not be confounded with the other.

Dr. MITCHELL has published several pretty songs which have been set to music and become popular. He has also given to the world a volume of poems, of which the longest was remarkable for an old-fashioned polish and vigour of versification. His MS. is rather graceful than picturesque or forcible—and these words apply equally well to his poetry in general. The signature indicates the hand.

General MORRIS has composed many songs which have taken fast hold upon the popular taste, and which are deservedly celebrated. He has caught the true *tone* for these things, and hence his popularity—a popularity which his enemies would fain make us believe is altogether attributable to his editorial influence. The charge is true only in a measure. The tone of which we speak is that kind of frank, free, hearty *sentiment* (rather than philosophy) which distinguishes Beranger, and which the critics, for want of a better term, call *nationality.*

His MS. is a simple unornamented hand, rather rotund than angular, very legible, forcible, and altogether in keeping with his style.

Mr. CALVERT was at one time principal editor of the " Baltimore American," and wrote for that journal some good paragraphs on the common topics of the day. He has also published many translations from the German, and one or two original poems—among others an imitation of Don Juan called " Pelayo," which did him no credit. He is essentially a feeble and commonplace writer of poetry, although his p prose compositions have a certain degree of merit. His chirography indicates the " commonplace" upon which we have commented. It is a very usual, scratchy, and tapering clerk's hand—a hand which no man of talent ever did or could indite, unless compelled by circumstances of more than ordinary force. The signature is far better than the general manuscript of his epistles.

Mr. McJILTON is better known from his contributions to the journals of the day than from any book-publications. He has much talent, and it is not improbable that he will hereafter distinguish himself, although as yet he has not composed anything of length which, as a whole, can be styled good. His MS. is not unlike that of Dr. Snodgrass, but it is somewhat clearer and better. We can predicate little respecting it beyond a love of exaggeration and *bizarrerie.*

Mr. GALLAGHER is chiefly known as a poet. He is the author of some of our most popular songs, and has written many long pieces of high but unequal merit. He has the true spirit, and will rise into a just distinction hereafter. His manuscript tallies well with our opinion. It is a very fine one—clear, bold, decided and picturesque. The signature above does not convey, in full force, the general character of his chirography, which is more rotund, and more decidedly placed upon the paper.

Mr. DANA ranks among our most eminent poets, and he has been the frequent subject of comment in our reviews. He has high qualities, undoubtedly, but his defects are many and great.

His MS. resembles that of Mr. Gallagher very nearly but is somewhat more rolling, and has less boldness and decision. The literary traits of the two gentlemen are very similar, although Mr. Dana is by far the more polished writer, and has a scholarship which Mr. Gallagher wants.

Mr. McMICHAEL is well known to the Philadelphia public by the number and force of his prose compositions, but he has seldom been tempted into book-publication. As a poet, he has produced some remarkably vigorous things. We have seldom seen a finer composition than a certain celebrated " Monody " of his.

His MS., when not hurried, is graceful and flowing, without picturesqueness. At times it is totally illegible. His chirography is one of those which have been so strongly modified by circumstances that it is nearly impossible to predicate anything with certainty respecting them.

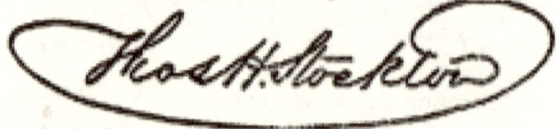

Mr. N. C. BROOKS has acquired some reputation as a Magazine writer. His serious prose is often very good—is always well-worded—but in his comic attempts he fails, without appearing to be aware of his failure. As a poet he has succeeded far better. In a work which he entitled " Scriptural Anthology" among many inferior compositions of length, there were several shorter pieces of great merit:—for example " Shelley's Obsequies" and " The Nicthanthes." Of late days we have seen little from his pen.

His MS. has much resemblance to that of Mr. Bryant, although altogether it is a better hand, with much more freedom and grace. With care Mr. Brooks can write a fine MS. just as with care he can compose a fine poem.

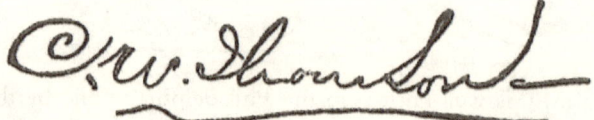

The Rev. THOMAS H. STOCKTON has written many pieces of fine poetry, and has lately distinguished himself as the editor of the " Christian World."

His MS. is fairly represented by his signature, and bears much resemblance to that of Mr. N. C. Brooks of Baltimore. Between these two gentlemen there exists also a remarkable similarity, not only of thought, but of personal bearing and character. We have already spoken of the peculiarities of Mr. B.'s chirography.

Mr. THOMSON has written many short poems, and some of them possess merit. They are characterised by tenderness and grace. His MS. has some resemblance to that of Professor Longfellow, and by many persons would be thought a finer hand. It is clear, legible, and open—what is called a rolling hand. It has too much tapering, and too much variation between the weight of the hair strokes and the downward ones, to be forcible or picturesque. In all those qualities which we have pointed out as especially distinctive of Professor Longfellow's M. it is remarkably deficient; and, in fact, the literary character of no two individuals could be more radically different.

The Reverend W. E. CHANNING is at the head of our moral and didactic writers. His reputation both at home and abroad is deservedly high, and in regard to the matters of purity, polish, and modulation of style, he may be said to have attained the dignity of a standard and a classic. He has, it is true, been severely criticised, even in respect to these very points, by the " Edinburgh Review." The critic, however, made out his case but lamely, and proved nothing beyond his own incompetence. To detect occasional or even frequent inadvertences in the way of bad grammar, faulty construction, or misusage of language, is not to prove impurity of *style*—a word which happily has a bolder signification than any dreamed of by the Zoilus of the Review in question. Style regards, more than anything else, the *tone* of a composition. All the rest is not unimportant, to be sure, but appertains to the minor morals of literature, and can be learned by rote by the meanest simpletons in letters—can be carried to its highest excellence by dolts, who, upon the whole, are despicable as stylists. Irving's style is inimitable in its grace and delicacy, yet few of our practised writers are guilty of more frequent inadvertences of language. In what may be termed his mere English, he is surpassed by fifty whom we could name. Mr. Tuckerman's English, on the contrary, is sufficiently pure, but a more lamentable style than that of his " Sicily" it would be difficult to point out.

Besides those peculiarities which we have already mentioned as belonging to Dr. Channing's style, we must not fail to mention a certain calm, broad deliberateness, which constitutes *force* in its highest character, and approaches to majesty. All these traits will be found to exist plainly in his chirography, the character of which is exemplified by the signature, although this is somewhat larger than the general manuscript.

Mr. WILMER has written and published much; but he has reaped the usual fruits of a spirit of independence, and thus failed to make that impression on the *popular* mind which his talents, under other circumstances, would have effected. But better days are in store for him, and for all who " hold to the right way," despising the yelping of the small dogs of our literature. His prose writings have all merit—always the merit of a chastened style. But he is more favourably known by his poetry, in which the student of the British classics will find much for warm admiration. We have few better versifiers than Mr. Wilmer.

His chirography plainly indicates the cautious polish and terseness of his style, but the signature does not convey the print-like appearance of the MS.

Mr. DOW is distinguished as the author of many fine sea-pieces, among which will be remembered a series of papers called " The Log of Old Ironsides." His land sketches are not generally so good. He has a fine imagination, which as yet is undisciplined, and leads him into occasional bombast. As a poet he has done better things than as a writer of prose.

His MS., which has been strongly modified by circumstances, gives no indication of his true character, literary or moral.

MR. WILD is well known as the present working editor of the New York " Tattler" and " Brother Jonathan." His attention was accidentally directed to literature about ten years ago, after a minority, to use his own words, " spent at sea, in a store, in a machine-shop, and in a printing-office." He is now, we believe, about thirty-one years of age. His deficiency of what is termed regular education would scarcely be gleaned from his editorials, which, in general, are unusually well written. His " Corrected Proofs" is a work which does him high credit, and which has been extensively circulated, although " printed at odd times by himself when he had nothing else to do."

His MS. resembles that of Joseph C. Neal in many respects, but is less open and less legible. His signature is altogether much better than his general chirography.

Mrs. ST. LEON LOUD is one of the finest poets of this country; possessing, we think, more of the true divine *afflatus* than any of her female contemporaries. She has, in especial, *imagination* of no common order, and unlike many of her sex whom we could mention, is not

Content to dwell in decencies forever.

While she *can*, upon occasion, compose the ordinary metrical sing-song with all the decorous proprieties which are in fashion, she yet ventures very frequently into a more ethereal region. We refer our readers to a truly beautiful little poem entitled the " Dream of the Lonely Isle," lately published in this Magazine.

Mrs. Loud's MS. is exceedingly clear, neat, and forcible, with just sufficient effeminacy and no more.

Pliny Earle.

Dr. PLINY EARLE, of Frankford, Pa, has not only distinguished himself by several works of medical and general science, but has become well known to the literary world, of late, by a volume of very fine poems, the longest, but by no means the best of which was entitled " Marathon." This latter is not greatly inferior to the " Marco Bozzaris" of Helleck, while some of the minor pieces equal any American poems. His chirography is peculiarly neat and beautiful, giving indication of the elaborate finish which characterises his compositions. The signature conveys the general hand.

David Hoffman.

DAVID HOFFMAN of Baltimore, has not only contributed much and well to monthly Magazines and Reviews, but has given to the world several valuable publications in book form. His style is terse, pungent, and otherwise excellent, although disfigured by a half-comic half-serious pedantry.

His MS. has about it nothing strongly indicative of character.

S. D. Langtree.

S. D. LANGTREE has been long and favourably known to the public as editor of the " Georgetown Metropolitan," and more lately of the " Democratic Review," both of which journals he has conducted with distinguished success. As a critic he has proved himself just, bold, and acute, while his prose compositions generally evince the man of talent and taste.

His MS. is not remarkably good, being somewhat too scratchy and tapering. We include him, of course, in the editorial category.

R. T. Conrad.

Judge CONRAD occupies, perhaps, the first place among our Philadelphia _literati_. He has distinguished himself both as a prose writer and a poet—not to speak of his high legal reputation. He has been a frequent contributor to the periodicals of this city, and we believe to one at least of the Eastern Reviews. His first production which attracted general notice was a tragedy entitled " Conrad, King of Naples." It was performed at the Arch Street Theatre, and elicited applause from the more judicious. This play was succeeded by " Jack Cade," performed at the Walnut Street Theatre, and lately modified and reproduced under the title of " Aylmere." In its new dress, this drama has been one of the most successful ever written by an American, not only attracting crowded houses, but extorting the good word of our best critics. In occasional poetry Judge Conrad has also done well. His lines " On a Blind Boy Soliciting Charity" have been greatly admired, and many of his other pieces evince ability of a high order. His political fame is scarcely a topic for these pages, and is, moreover, too much a matter of common observation to need comment from us.

His MS. is neat, legible, and forcible, evincing combined caution and spirit in a very remarkable degree.

The chirography of Ex-President ADAMS (whose poem, " The Wants of Man," has of late attracted so much attention), is remarkable for a certain steadiness of purpose pervading the whole, and overcoming even the constitutional tremulousness of the writer's hand. wavering in every letter, the entire MS. has yet a firm, regular, and decisive appearance. It is also very legible.

P. P. COOKE of Winchester, Virginia, is well known, especially in the South, as the author of numerous excellent contributions to the " Southern Literary Messenger." He has written some of the finest poetry of which America can boast. A little piece of his, entitled " Florence Vane" and contributed to the " Gentleman's Magazine" of this city, during our editorship of that journal, was remarkable for the high ideality it evinced, and for the great delicacy and melody of its rhythm. It was universally admired and copied, as well here as in England. We saw it not long ago, *as original,* in " Bentley's Miscellany." Mr. Cooke has, we believe, nearly ready for press a novel called " Maurice Werterbern," whose success we predict with confidence. His MS. is clear, forcible, and legible, but disfigured by some little of that affectation which is scarcely a blemish in his literary style.

Mr. J. BEAUCHAMP JONES has been, we believe, connected for many years past with the lighter literature of Baltimore, and at present edits the " Baltimore Saturday Visitor," with much judgment and general ability. He is the author of a series of papers of high merit now in course of publication in the " Visitor," and entitled " Wild Western Scenes."

His MS. is distinct, and might be termed a fine one; but is somewhat too much in consonance with the ordinary clerk style to be either graceful or forcible.

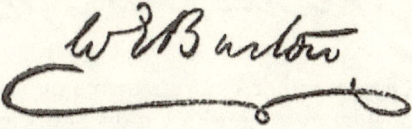

Mr. BURTON is better known as a comedian than as a literary man, but he has written many short prose articles of merit., and his quondam editorship of the " Gentleman's Magazine" would, at all events, entitle him to a place in this collection. He has, moreover, published one or two books. An annual issued by Carey and Hart in 1840 consisted entirely of prose contributions from himself, with poetical ones from Charles West Thompson, Esq. In this work many of the tales were good.

Mr. Burton's MS. is scratchy and *petite*, betokening indecision and care or caution.

RICHARD HENRY WILDE of Georgia, has acquired much reputation as a poet, and especially as the author of a little piece entitled " My Life is like the Summer Rose," whose claim to originality has been made the subject of repeated and reiterated attack and defence. Upon the whole it is hardly worth quarrelling about. Far better verses are to be found in every second newspaper we take up. Mr. Wilde has also lately published, or is about to publish, a " Life of Tasso," for which he has been long collecting material.

His MS. has all the peculiar sprawling and elaborate tastelessness of Mr. Palfrey's, to which altogether it bears a marked resemblance. The love of effect, however, is more perceptible in Mr. Wilde's than even in Mr. Palfrey's.

LEWIS CASS, the Ex-Secretary of War, has distinguished himself as one of the finest *belles-lettres* scholars of America. At one period he was a very regular contributor to the " Southern Literary Messenger," and even lately he has furnished that journal with one or two very excellent papers.

His MS. is clear, deliberate, and statesmanlike; resembling that of Edward Everett very closely. It is not often that we see a letter written altogether by himself.

He generally employs an amanuensis, whose chirography does not differ materially from his own, but is somewhat more regular.

Mr. JAMES BROOKS enjoys rather a private than a public literary reputation; but his talents are unquestionably great, and his productions have been numerous and excellent. As the author of many of the celebrated " Jack Downing" letters, and as the reputed author of the whole of them, he would at all events be entitled to a place among our *literati*.

His chirography is simple, clear, and legible, with little grace and less boldness. These traits are precisely those of his literary style.

As the authorship of the " Jack Downing" letters is even still considered by many a moot point (although in fact there should be no question about it), and as we have already given the signature of Mr. Seba Smith, and (just above) of Mr. Brooks, we now present our readers with a facsimile signature of the " *veritable Jack* " himself, written by him individually in our own bodily presence. Here, then, is an opportunity of comparison.

The chirography of " the veritable Jack" is a very good, honest sensible hand, and not very dissimilar to that of Ex. President Adams.

Mr. J. R. LOWELL, of Massachusetts, is entitled, in our opinion, to at least the second or third place among the poets of America. We say this on account of the vigour of his *imagination*—a faculty to be first considered in all, criticism upon poetry. In this respect he surpasses, we think, any of our writers (at least any of those who have put themselves prominently forth as poets) with the exception of Longfellow, and perhaps one other. His ear for rhythm, nevertheless, is imperfect, and he is very far from possessing the artistic ability of either Longfellow, Bryant, Halleck, Sprague, or Pierpont. The reader desirous of properly estimating the powers of Mr. Lowell will find a very beautiful little poem from his pen in the October number of this Magazine. There is one also (not quite so fine) in the number for last month. He will contribute regularly.

His MS. is strongly indicative of the vigour and precision of his poetical thought. The man who writes thus, for example, will never be guilty of metaphorical extravagance, and there will be found *terseness* as well as strength in all that he does.

Mr. L. J. CIST, of Cincinnati, has not written much prose, and is known especially by his poetical compositions. many of which have been very popular, although they are at times disfigured by false metaphor, and by a meretricious straining after effect. This latter foible makes itself clearly apparent in his chirography, which abounds in ornamental flourishes, not ill executed, to be sure, but in very bad taste.

Mr. ARTHUR is not without a rich talent for description of scenes in low life, but is uneducated, and too fond of mere vulgarities to please a refined taste. He has published " The Subordinate," and " Insubordination," two tales distinguished by the peculiarities above mentioned. He has also written much for our weekly papers and the " Lady's Book."

His hand is a commonplace clerk's hand, such as we might expect him to write. The signature is much better than the general MS.

Mr. HEATH is almost the only person of any literary distinction residing in the chief city of the Old Dominion. He edited the " Southern Literary Messenger" in the five or six first months of its existence; and, since the secession of the writer of this article, has frequently aided in its editorial conduct. He is the author of " Edge-Hill," a well written novel, which, owing to the circumstances of its publication, did not meet with the reception it deserved: His writings are rather polished and graceful than forcible or original, and these peculiarities can be traced in his chirography.

Dr. THOMAS HOLLEY CHIVERS, of New York, is at the same time one of the best and one of the worst poets in America. His productions affect one as a wild dream strange, incongruous, full of images of more than arabesque monstrosity, and snatches of sweet ill-sustained song. Even his worst nonsense (and some of it is horrible) has an indefinite charm of sentiment and melody. We can never be sure that there is *any* meaning in his words—neither is there any meaning in many of our finest musical airs—but the effect is very similar in both. His figures of speech are metaphor run mad, and his grammar is often none at all. Yet there are as fine individual passages to be found in the poems of Dr. Chivers as in those of any poet whatsoever.

His MS. resembles that of P. P. Cooke very nearly, and in poetical character the two gentlemen are closely akin. If Cooke is, by much, the more *correct,* while Dr. Chivers is sometimes the more poetic. Mr. C. always sustains himself; Dr. C. never.

Judge STORY, and his various literary and political labours, are too well known to require comment.

His chirography is a noble one—bold, clear, massive, and deliberate, betokening in the most unequivocal manner all the characteristics of his intellect. The plain unornamented style of his compositions is impressed with accuracy upon his handwriting, the whole air of which is well conveyed in the signature.

Mr. JOHN FROST, Professor of Belles Lettres. in the High School of Philadelphia, and at present editor of " The Young People's Book," has distinguished himself by numerous literary compositions for the periodicals of the day, and by a great number of published works which come under the head of the *utile* rather than of the *dulce*— at least in the estimation of the young. He is a gentleman of fine taste, sound scholarship, and great general ability.

His chirography denotes his mental idiosyncrasy with great precision. Its careful neatness, legibility, and finish are but a part of that turn of mind which leads him so frequently into compilation. The signature here given is more diminutive than usual.

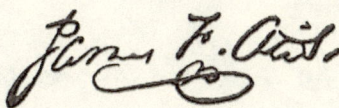

Mr. J. F. OTIS is well known as a writer for the Magazines; and has, at various times, been connected with many of the leading newspapers of the day—especially with those in New York and Washington. His prose and poetry are equally good; but he writes too much and too hurriedly to write invariably well. His taste is fine, and his judgment in literary matters is to be depended upon at all times when not interfered with by his personal antipathies, or predilections.

His chirography is exceedingly illegible and, like his style, has every possible fault except that of the commonplace.

Mr. REYNOLDS occupied at one time a distinguished position in the eye of the public on account of his great and laudable exertions to get up the American South Polar expedition, from a personal participation in which he was most shamefully excluded. He has written much and well. Among other works, the public are indebted to him for a graphic account of the noted voyage of the frigate Potomac to Madagascar.

His MS. is an ordinary clerk's hand, giving no indication of character.

DAVID PAUL BROWN is scarcely more distinguished in his legal capacity than by his literary compositions. As a dramatic writer he has met with much success. His " Sertorius" has been particularly well received both upon the stage and in the closet. His fugitive productions, both in prose and verse, have also been numerous, diversified, and excellent.

His chirography has no doubt been strongly modified by the circumstances of his position. No one can expect a lawyer in full practice to give in his MS. any true indication of his intellect or character.

E. C. Stedman

Mrs. E. CLEMENTINE STEDMAN has lately attracted much attention by the delicacy and grace of her poetical compositions, as well as by the piquancy and spirit of her prose. For some months past we have been proud to rank her among the best of the contributors to " Graham's Magazine."

Her chirography differs as materially from that of her sex in general as does her literary manner from the usual namby-pamby of our blue-stockings. It is indeed a beautiful MS., very closely resembling that of Professor Longfellow, but somewhat more diminutive, and far more full of grace.

John G. Whittier

J. GREENLEAF WHITTIER is placed by his particular admirers in the very front rank of American poets. We are not disposed, however, to agree with their decision in every respect. Mr. Whittier is a fine versifier, so far as strength is regarded independently of modulation. His subjects, too, are usually chosen with the view of affording scope to a certain *vivida vis* of expression which seems to be his forte; but in taste, and especially in *imagination,* which Coleridge has justly styled the *soul* of all poetry, he is ever remarkably deficient. His themes are *never* to our liking.

His chirography is an ordinary clerk's hand, affording little indication of character.

Ann S. Stephens

Mrs. ANN S. STEPHENS was at one period the editor of the " Portland Magazine," a periodical of which we have not heard for some time, and which, we presume, has been discontinued. More lately her name has been placed upon the title-page of " The Lady's Companion" of New York: as one of the conductors of that journal—to which she has contributed many articles of merit and popularity. She has also written much and well for various other periodicals, and will hereafter enrich this magazine with her compositions, and act as one of its editors.

Her MS. is a very excellent one, and differs from that of her sex in general by an air of more than usual force and freedom.

Note—The foregoing "Chapter On Autography," as will be seen from a reference in the opposite page, originally appeared in two parts.—*Ed.*

APPENDIX.

In the foregoing *facsimile* signatures of the most distinguished American *literati* our design was to furnish a *complete* series of Autographs, embracing a specimen of the MS. of *each of the most noted among our living male and female writers,* For obvious reasons, we made no attempt at classification or arrangement—either in reference to reputation or our own private opinion of merit. Our second article will be found to contain as many of the *Dii majorum gentium* as our first ; and this, our third and last as many as either—although fewer names, upon the whole, than the preceding papers. The impossibility of procuring the signatures now given, at a period sufficiently early for the immense edition of December, has obliged us to introduce this Appendix.

It is with great pleasure that we have found our anticipations fulfilled in respect to the *popularity* of these chapters —our individual claim to merit is so trivial that we may be permitted to say so much—but we confess it was with no less surprise than pleasure that we observed so little discernment of opinion manifested in relation to the hasty critical, or rather gossiping, observations which accompanied the signatures. Where the subject was so wide and so necessarily *personal*—where the claims of more than one hundred *literati*, summarily disposed of, were turned over for re-adjudication to a press so intricately bound up in their interest as is ours—it is really surprising how little of dissent was mingled with so much of general comment. The fact, however, speaks loudly to one point:—to the *unity of truth.* It assures us that the differences which exist among us are differences not of real, but of affected opinion, and that the voice of him who maintains fearlessly what he believes honestly, is pretty sure to find an echo (if the speaking be not mad) in the vast heart of the world at large.

The " Writings of CHARLES SPRAGUE" were first collected and published about nine months ago by Mr. Charles S. Francis of New York. At the time of the issue of the book we expressed our opinion frankly in respect to the general merits of the author—an opinion with which one or two members of the Boston press did not see fit to agree—but which, as yet, we have found no reason for modifying. What we say now is, in spirit, merely a repetition of what we said then. Mr. Sprague is an accomplished *belles-lettres* scholar, so far as the usual ideas of scholarship extend. He is a very correct rhetorician of the old school. His versification has not been equaled by that of any American—has been surpassed by no one living or dead. In this regard there are to be found finer passages in his poems than any elsewhere. These are his chief merits. In the *essentials* of poetry he is excelled by twenty of our countrymen whom we could name. Except in a very few instances he gives no evidence of the loftier ideality. His " Winged Worshippers" and " Lines on the Death of M. S. C." are *beautiful* poems—but he has written nothing else which should be called so. His " Shakspeare Ode," upon which his high reputation mainly depended, is quite a *second-hand* affair—with no merit whatever beyond that of a polished and vigorous versification. Its imitation of " Collins' Ode to the Passions" is obvious. Its allegorical conduct is mawkish, *passé*, and absurd. The poem, upon the whole, is just such a one as would have obtained its author an Etonian prize some forty or fifty years ago. It is an exquisite specimen of mannerism, without meaning and without merit—of an artificial, but most inartistical style of composition, of which conventionality is the soul,—taste, nature, and reason the antipodes. A man may be a clever financier without being a genius.

It requires out little effort to see in Mr. Sprague's MS. all the idiosyncrasy of his intellect. Here are distinctness, precision, and vigour—but vigour employed upon *grace* rather than upon its legitimate functions. The signature fully indicates the general hand—in which the spirit of elegant imitation and conservatism may be seen reflected as in a mirror.

[signature: Cornelius Mathews]

Mr.. CORNELIUS MATHEWS is one of the editors of " Arcturus," a monthly journal which has attained much reputation during the brief period of its existence. He is the author of " Puffer Hopkins," a clever satirical tale somewhat given to excess in caricature, and also of the well written retrospective criticisms which appear in his Magazine. He is better known, however, by " The Motley Book," published some years ago—a work which we had no opportunity of reading. He is a gentleman of taste and judgment unquestionably.

His MS. is much to our liking—bold, distinct, and picturesque—such a hand as no one destitute of talent indites. The signature conveys the hand.

[signature: Charles Fenno Hoffman]

Mr. CHARLES FENNO HOFFMAN is the author of " A Winter in the West," " Greyslaer," and other productions of merit. At one time he edited, with much ability, the " American Monthly Magazine" in conjunction with Mr. Benjamin, and subsequently with Dr. Bird. He is a gentle man of talent. His chirography is not unlike that of Mr. Mathews. It has the same boldness, strength, and picturesqueness, but is more diffuse, more ornamented, and less legible. Our *facsimile* is from a somewhat hurried signature, which fails in giving a correct idea of the general hand.

[signature: Horace Greeley]

Mr. HORACE GREELEY, present editor of " The Tribune," and formerly of the " New-Yorker," has for many years been remarked as one of the most able and honest of American editors. He has written much and invariably well. His political knowledge is equal to that of any of his contemporaries—his general information extensive. As a *belles lettres* critic he is entitled to high respect.

His MS. is a remarkable one—having about it a peculiarity which we know not how better to designate than as a *converse* of the picturesque. His characters are scratchy and irregular, ending with an *abrupt tapering* we may be allowed this contradiction in terms, where we have the *facsimile* to prove that there is no contradiction in fact. All abrupt MSS., save this, have square or *concise* terminations of the letters. The whole chirography puts us in mind of a *jig*. We can fancy the writer jerking up his hand from the paper at the end of each word, and, indeed, of each letter. What mental idiosyncrasy lies *perdu* beneath all this is more than we can say, but we will venture to assert that Mr. Greeley (whom we do not know personally) is, *personally,* a very remarkable man.

The name of Mr. PROSPER M. WETMORE is familiar to all readers of American light literature. He has written a great deal, at various periods, both in prose and poetry (but principally in the latter) for our Papers, Magazines, and Annuals. Of late days we have seen but little, comparatively speaking, from his pen.

His MS. is not unlike that of Fitz-Greene Halleck, but is by no means so good. Its clerky flourishes indicate a love of the beautiful with an undue straining for effect—qualities which are distinctly traceable in his poetic efforts. As many as five or six words are occasionally run together; and no man who writes thus will be noted for *finish* of style. Mr. Wetmore is sometimes very slovenly in his best compositions.

Professor WARE, of Harvard, has written some very excellent poetry, but is chiefly known by his " Life of the Saviour," " Hints on Extemporaneous Preaching," and other religious works.

His MS. is fully shown in the signature. It evinces the direct unpretending strength and simplicity which characterise the man, not less than his general compositions.

The name of WILLIAM B. O. PEABODY, like that of Mr. Wetmore, is known chiefly to the readers of our light literature, and much more familiarly to Northern than to Southern readers. He is a resident of Springfield, Mass. His occasional poems have been much admired.

His chirography is what would be called beautiful by the ladies universally, and, perhaps, by a large majority of the bolder sex. Individually, we think it a miserable one—too careful, undecided, tapering, and effeminate. It is not unlike Mr. Paulding's, but is more regular and more legible, with less force. We hold it as undeniable that no man of *genius* ever wrote such a hand.

EPES SARGENT, Esq., has acquired high reputation as the author of " Velasco," a tragedy full of beauty as a poem, but not adapted—perhaps not intended—for representation. He has written, besides, many very excellent poems—" The Missing Ship," for example, published in the " Knickerbocker"—the " Night Storm at Sea"—and, especially, a fine production entitled " Shells and Sea-Weeds." One or two Theatrical Addresses from his pen are very creditable *in their way*—but the way itself is, as we have before said, execrable. As an editor, Mr. Sargent has also distinguished himself. He is a gentleman of taste and high talent.

His MS. is too much in the usual clerk style to be either vigorous, graceful, or easily read. It resembles Mr. Wetmore's, but has somewhat more force. The signature is better than the general hand, but conveys its idea very well.

The name of "WASHINGTON ALLSTON," the poet and painter, is one that has been long before the public. Of his paintings we have here nothing to say—except briefly, that the most noted of them are not to our taste. His poems are not all of a high order of merit; and, in truth, the faults of his pencil and of his pen are identical. Yet every reader will remember his " Spanish Maid" with pleasure, and the " Address to Great Britain," first published in Coleridge's " Sibylline Leaves," and attributed to an English author, is a production of which Mr. Allston may be proud.

His MS., notwithstanding an exceedingly simple and boyish air, is one which we particularly admire. It is forcible, picturesque, and legible, without ornament of any description. Each letter is formed with a thorough distinctness and individuality. Such a MS. indicates caution and precision, most unquestionably—but we say of it as we say of Mr. Peabody's (a very different MS.) that no man of original genius ever did or could habitually indite it under any circumstances whatever. The signature conveys the general hand with accuracy.

MR. ALFRED B. STREET has been long before the public as a poet. At as early an age as fifteen, some of his pieces were published by Mr. Bryant in the " Evening Post"—among these was one of much merit, entitled a " Winter Scene." In the " New-York Book," and in the collections of American poetry by Messieurs Keese and Bryant, will be found many excellent specimens of his maturer powers. " The Willewemoc," " The Forest Tree," " The Indian's Vigil," " The Lost Hunter," and

" White Lake" we prefer to any of his other productions which have met our eye. Mr. Street has fine taste, and a keen sense of the beautiful. He writes carefully, elaborately, and correctly. He has made Mr. Byrant his model, and in, all of Byrant's good points would be nearly his equal, were it not for the sad and too perceptible stain of the imitation. That he has imitated at all—or rather that, in mature age, he has persevered in his imitations—is sufficient warranty for placing him among the men of talent rather than among the men of genius.

His MS. is full corroboration of this warranty. It is very pretty chirography, graceful, legible, and neat. By most persons it would be called beautiful. The fact is, it is without fault—but its merits, like those of his poems, are chiefly negative.

Mr. RICHARD PENN SMITH, although perhaps better known in Philadelphia than elsewhere, has acquired much literary reputation. His chief works are " The Forsaken," a novel; a pseudo-autobiography called " Colonel Crockett's Tour in Texas;" the tragedy of " Caius Marius," and two domestic dramas entitled " The Disowned" and " The Deformed." He has also published two volumes of miscellanies under the title of " The Actress of Padua and other Tales," besides occasional poetry. We are not sufficiently cognisant of any of these works to speak with decision respecting their merits. In a biography of Mr. Smith, however, very well written, by his friend, Mr. McMichael, of this city, we are informed of " The Forsaken" that " a large edition of it was speedily exhausted"—of " The Actress of Padua," that it "had an extensive sale and was much commended" —of the "Tour in Texas," that " few books attained an equal popularity"—of " Caius Marius," that "it has great capabilities for an acting play,"—of " The Disowned" and " The Deformed," that they "were performed at the London theatres, where they both made a favourable impression" and of his poetry in general, " that it will be found superior to the average quality of that commodity." " It is by his dramatic efforts," says the biographer, " that his merits as a poet must be determined, and judged by these he will be assigned a place in the foremost rank of American writers." We have only to add that we have the highest respect for the judgment of Mr. McMichael.

Mr. Smith's MS. is clear, graceful, and legible, and would generally be called a fine hand, but is somewhat too clerky for our taste.

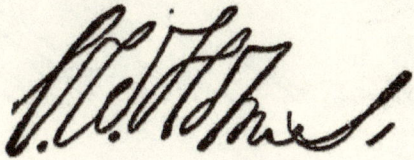

Dr. OLIVER WENDEL HOLMES, of Boston, late Professor of Anatomy and Physiology at Dartmouth College, has written many productions of merit, and has been pronounced by a very high authority the best of the humorous poets of the day.

His chirography is remarkably fine, and a quick fancy might easily detect, in its graceful yet picturesque quaintness, an analogy with the vivid drollery of his style. The signature is a fair specimen of the general MS.

Bishop DOANE, of New Jersey, is somewhat more extensively known in his clerical than in a literary capacity, but has accomplished much more than sufficient in the world of books to entitle him to a place among the most noted of our living men of letters. The compositions by which he is best known were published, we believe, during his professorship of Rhetoric and Belles Lettres in Washington College, Hartford.

His MS. has some resemblance to that of Mr. Greeley of " The Tribune." The signature is far bolder and altogether better than the general hand.

We believe that Mr. ALBERT PIKE has never published poems in book form; nor has he written anything since 1834. His " Hymns to the Gods," and " Ode to the Mocking_Bird," being printed in " Blackwood," are the chief basis of his reputation. His lines " To Spring" are, however, much better in every respect, and a little poem from his pen, entitled " Ariel" originally published in the " Boston Pearl," is one of the finest of American compositions. Mr. Pike has unquestionably merit, and that of a high order. His ideality is rich and well-disciplined. He is the most *classic* of our poets in the best sense of the term, and of course his classicism is very different from that of Mr. Sprague—to whom, nevertheless, he bears much resemblance in other respects. Upon the whole, there are few of our native writers to whom we consider him inferior.

His MS. shows clearly the spirit of his intellect. We observe in it a keen sense not only of the beautiful and graceful but of the picturesque-neatness, precision, and general finish, verging upon effeminacy. In force it is deficient. The signature fails to convey the entire MS., which depends upon masses for its peculiar character.

James McHenry

Dr. JAMES MCHENRY, of Philadelphia, is well known to the literary world as the writer of numerous articles in our Reviews and lighter journals, but more especially as the author of " The Antediluvians," an epic poem which has been the victim of a most shameful cabal in this country, and the subject of a very disgraceful pasquinade on the part of Professor Wilson. Whatever may be the demerits, in some regard, of this poem, there can be no question of the utter want of fairness, and even of common decency, which distinguished the Philippic in question. The writer of a *just* review of the " Antediluvians"—the only tolerable American epic—would render an important service to the literature of his country.

Dr. McHenry's MS. is distinct: bold, and simple, without ornament or superfluity. The signature well conveys the idea of the general hand.

R. S. Nichols

Mrs. R. S. NICHOLS has acquired much reputation in late years by frequent and excellent contributions to the Magazines and Annuals. Many of her compositions will be found in our pages.

Her MS. is fair, neat, and legible, but formed somewhat too much upon the ordinary boarding-school model to afford any indication of character. The signature is a good specimen of the hand.

Rich. A. Locke

Mr. RICHARD ADAMS LOCKE is one among the few men of *unquestionable genius* whom the country possesses. Of the " Moon Hoax" it is supererogatory to say one word—not to know *that* argues one's self unknown. Its rich imagination will long dwell in the memory of everyone who read it, and surely if

the worth of any thing
is just so much as it will bring—

if, in short, we are to judge of the value of a literary composition in any degree by its *effect*—then was the " Hoax" most precious.

But Mr. Locke is also a poet of high order. We have seen—nay more—we have heard him read—verses of his own which would make the fortune of two-thirds of our poetasters; and he is yet so modest as never to have published a volume of poems. As an editor—as a political writer—as a writer in general—we think that he has scarcely a superior in America. There is no man among us to whose sleeve we would rather pin—not our *faith* (of that we say nothing)—but our *judgment*.

His MS. is clear, hold, and forcible—somewhat modified, no doubt, by the circumstances of his editorial position but still sufficiently indicative of his fine intellect.

Mr. RALPH WALDO EMERSON belongs to a class of gentlemen with whom we have no patience whatever—the mystics for mysticism's sake. Quintilian mentions a pedant who taught obscurity, and who once said to a pupil " this is excellent, for I do not understand it myself". How the good man would have chuckled over Mr. E! His present *role* seems to be the out-Carlyling Carlyle. *Lycophron Tenebrosus* is a fool to him. The best answer to his twaddle is *cui bono?*—a very little Latin phrase very generally mistranslated and misunderstood—*cui bono ?*—to whom is it a benefit? If not to Mr. Emerson individually, then surely to no man living.

His love of the obscure does not prevent him, nevertheless, from the composition of occasional poems in which beauty is apparent *by flashes*. Several of his effusions appeared in the " Western Messenger"—more in the " Dial," of which he is the soul—or the sun—or the shadow. We remember the " Sphynx," the " Problem," the " Snow Storm," and some fine old-fashioned verses entitled " Oh fair and stately maid whose eye."

His MS. is bad, sprawling, illegible, and irregular—although sufficiently bold. This latter trait may be, and no doubt is, only a portion of his general affectation.

A Biographical Dictionary of Poe's Subjects

The guide that follows is intended to provide basic identification of the figures Poe mentions. The intent here is to give a basic sense of who each person was, not to provide anything like a complete biography of each individual. The length of the entries varies, sometimes because of the available source material, sometimes because it seemed more useful to enumerate works for certain writers than for others. In general, this guide will probably be more useful in introducing obscure figures than as a reference to those for whom information is readily available elsewhere. In either case, the reader is encouraged to use this reference as a starting point for more extensive research.

Poe's claim that "we confine ourselves *to the most noted among the living literati of the country*" was disputed even at the time. In a few cases, Poe says himself that the person has published little. Still, the great majority of the people mentioned had at least some reputation at the time and many were then very well known. Of the latter, a minority still have major reputations (Longfellow, Emerson, etc.). Others are known to scholars of the period but not to the general public. Most of Poe's subjects have left some significant trace, if only in documents that reference the period. In just a few cases, almost no information seems to be available today.

Even a casual glance at the entries that follow will show that the great majority of these writers had other careers, most frequently as lawyers and/or clergymen, sometimes as doctors, professors and/or military officers, and often several at the same time or successively. Also, many of the same people worked as journalists, even while maintaining their other career(s). A number of names of periodicals also recur in these entries: *The Southern Literary Messenger, Godey's Lady's Book, Graham's Magazine,* etc. Poe and his friends wrote for many of these and sometimes edited them as well. Separate guides exist (on-line and in print) of all the different periodicals mentioned and their place in the literary life of the time. For those who care to delve deeper, the information in such lists, taken together with the biographical information here, offers a panorama of the literary life of the time.

I

ADAMS, John Quincy 1767-1848 – The sixth president of the United States. A blunt, determined and brilliant man, he served his country in a range of different capacities, including diplomatic missions abroad, but was often unpopular. As Secretary of State, he negotiated the transfer of Florida to the United States. He has been credited as the author of "The Monroe Doctrine'. His election as president was tightly contested and ultimately decided in the House of Representatives. From 1831 until his death he served in Congress, a fierce opponent of slavery. His final words were, ""This is the last of earth; I am content."

ALLSTON, Washington 1779-1843 - An American painter who lived in England from 1811 to 1818. He opened a studio in Boston in 1818 and produced numerous works well-known at the time. Some called him the "American Titian", because of his abilities as a colorist. He also wrote poems such as "The Sylphs of the Seasons," (1809), "The Paint King" and "The Two Painters, "the romance *Monaldi* (1841), and *Lectures on Art, and Poems* (1850).

ANTHON, Charles 1797-1867 - Professor of Greek and Latin at Columbia where he taught from 1820-57. An associate of the Mormon Church, asked him to authenticate writings Joseph Smith had presented as 'Reformed Egyptian'. Anthon later strongly denied he had done so. This was in keeping with his nickname – 'Bull' –, but contradicts Poe's comments about his 'want of force'. In 1837, Poe copied Hebrew letters and Anthon's interpretations of them and presented them as his own.

ARTHUR, Timothy Shay 1809-1885 - Having edited *The Athenaeum* in Baltimore, he founded *Arthur's Home Magazine* in 1852 and ran it thereafter. His moralizing tales of domestic life which were very popular and, with W. H. Carpenter, histories of the states of the union. His works include *Lights and Shadows of Real Life*, *Tales for Rich and Poor*, *Library for the Household*, *Ten Nights in a Bar-Room*, and *Steps to Heaven*, as well as *The Good Time Coming* (1855), said to verge "on spiritualism and Swedenborgianism".

BENJAMIN, Park 1809-1864 – Lawyer, poet and one of the first editors of the *New England Magazine*. Worked with Charles Fenno Hoffman on the *American Monthly Magazine* (1837) with Horace Greeley on the *New-Yorker*, then on *Brother Jonathan*, a literary weekly paper. In 1840, he started the *New World*, working with Epes Sargent

and Rufus W. Griswold. *The Meditation of Nature* (1832), *Poetry, a Satire*, (1832), and *Infatuation* (1844), are the best known of his longer poems. "The Tired Hunter," "The Nautilus," "To One Beloved," "The Departed," and "The Old Sexton"are the most successful of his shorter poems.

BIRD, Robert Montgomery 1806-1854 – A novelist and dramatist who was briefly a doctor. His drama *The Gladiator* (1832) attacked slavery by portraying a Roman slave revolt. His plays *Oraliloossa* (1832) and *The Broker of Bogota* (1834) were set in South America. He was popular as novelist, and wrote the novels *Calavar* (1834), *The Infidel* (1835) and *Nick of the Woods* (1837). He later became literary editor and part owner of a newspaper.

BROOKS, James 1810-1873 - A Maine journalist who began as a lawyer, he went to Washington in 1832 for the *Portland Advertiser*. He then wrote a series of letters from Creek, Cherokee and Choctaw country in Georgia and Alabama, just at the time these tribes were being forced west. In 1836, he established the *Express* in New York. He served in the New York legislature and then in Congress from 1843 to 1873, when he was censured for his dealings with the railroad. In 1871-2, he had traveled around the world and wrote about his trip in the *Express* and in *A Seven Months' Run, Up and Down and Around the World* (1872).

BROOKS, Nathan Covington 1819-1898 - A noted educator, he organized the Baltimore female college in 1848. Aside from a number of Latin and Greek textbooks, he wrote various occasional poems, such as "Shelley's Obsequies" and "The Fall of Superstition". His *Complete History of the Mexican War* (1849) was once considered a standard work.

BROWN, David Paul 1795-1872 - A Philadelphia orator and lawyer. Though very successful, he spent a good income over-generously. He supposedly wrote his tragedy *Sertorius, or the Roman Patriot* (1830) on evening horseback rides. This and other works for the stage were not successful. He also wrote *The Forum, or Forty Years' Full Practice at the Philadelphia Bar* (1856) and *The Press, the Politician, the People, and the Judiciary* (1869) His son, Robert Eden, edited and published *The Forensic Speeches of David Paul Brown* (1873).

BROWNSON, Orestes Augustus 1803-1876 - He went through numerous belief systems, including several Christian denominations and a variety of Socialism, rejecting Christianity and then serving as a pastor, before becoming a Catholic in 1844. This history was reviewed in his *The Convert; or, Leaves from my Experience* (1857). He also edited and founded a number of publications, including *The Boston Quarterly Review* (1838). His positions on Christianity, property and slavery led to various conflicts and controversies over his life.

BRYANT, William Cullen 1794-1878 – Poet and journalist. He published his first book of verse, *The Embargo, or Sketches of the Times; A Satire by a Youth of thirteen*, in 1808. His most famous poem, "Thanatopsis" (1817) appeared while he was still practicing as a lawyer. In 1821, he published *Poems*, which included the famous "To a Waterfowl". From 1826 to 1829, he became editor and then chief owner of the *New York Evening Post*. Though he was a celebrated poet, his association with the paper and its political stances then dominated the rest of his life.

BURTON, William Evans 1804-1860 - English actor who came to the United States in 1834 and established New York's celebrated Chambers Street Theatre in 1848. Burton himself was successful in a wide range of parts from Shakespeare, Dickens and other authors. He wrote "The Actor's Soliloquy" and "Waggeries and Vagaries" and edited the *Literary Souvenir* in 1838 and 1840. In 1837, he established *The Gentleman's Magazine*, of which Poe was briefly assistant editor (1840). He also published a *Cyclopedia of Wit and Humor* (1858).

CALVERT, George Henry 1803-1889 - A great-grandson of Lord Baltimore; his works were once widely known. Editor of the *Baltimore American* for several years. Having moved to Newport, Rhode Island in 1843, he became mayor in 1853. He wrote a number of biographies, books of poetry and essays, as well as *Illustrations of Phrenology* (1832).

CASS, Lewis 1782-1866 - He began as a lawyer in Ohio, was elected to the legislature and subsequently served both in government and the military, notably in the War of 1812. As civil governor of Michigan he arranged treaties ceding Indian land to the United States while, over eighteen years, building up an administrative infrastructure. Accounts of an 1820 expedition to the headwaters of the Mississippi, published in the *North American Review* several years later, added to his fame. Subsequently, he was much involved in politics and other military conflicts. He also published *Inquiries concerning the History, Traditions, and Languages of the Indians living within the United States* (1823)

and *France, its King, Court, and Government* (1840).

CHANDLER, Joseph Ripley 1792-1880 – From 1822 to 1826, he revived the *United States Gazette* and remained with the paper, a prominent Whig journal, until 1847. He was a Whig member of Congress (1849-1855), then minister to the Two Sicilies. Very interested in prison reform, he wrote on that as well as other subjects, including grammar, in a *Grammar of the English Language* (1821).

CHANNING, William Ellery 1780-1842 - A New England clergyman, and a compelling orator, increasingly involved with the anti-slavery cause. He became known – apparently despite himself – as the leader of the Unitarians in the 20's and 30's. His essays in the *North American Review* and the *Christian Review* gained him a wide literary reputation. His writings on slavery include *The Slavery Question* (1839), a tract on "Emancipation" (1840), and a piece on "The Duty of the Free States" (1842), which addressed the case of slaves who had seized the brig "Creole," and brought it to Nassau.

CHIVERS, Thomas Holley 1807-1897 - A Georgia doctor, he wrote poems said to have influenced Swinburne and Rosetti. Two of his poems, "To Allegra Florence" and "Isadore", have been suggested as models for "The Raven". *The last pleiad and other poems* (1845) was his most popular work. He wrote a *Life* of Edgar Allen Poe, as well as articles trying to show Poe's debt to his own work.

CIST, Lewis Jacob 1818-1885 – Banker, poet and collector of autographs and portraits. Already as a boy he wrote poetry and music. He wrote for the *Western Monthly Magazine*, *Hesperian*, and *Cist's Weekly Advertiser*, and for several years, h published the *Souvenir*, the first annual of the West. Poe, reviewing his collected *Poems* (1845) in the *Broadway Journal* wrote that Cist had many admirers. He is virtually unknown today.

CONRAD, Judge Robert Taylor 1810-1858 - A poet, lawyer, judge, editor and public speaker, he published the tragedy *Conradin* before he was twenty-one. Between sitting on the bench and editing or publishing several periodicals (including *Graham's Magazine*), he wrote tragedies, including *Aylmere* and *The Heretic*. His collection *Ayhnere, or the Bondmand of Kent, and other Poems* (1852) includes "The Sons of the Wilderness", on the plight of Native Americans.

COOKE, Philip Pendleton 1816–1850 - A Virginian poet and lawyer, he loved practical pursuits such as hunting and fishing. Reviewing Poe's work, he said he hoped to read "one cheerful book made by his imagination" (!). Most known for the *Froissart Ballads*, he wrote both prose and poetry for the *Knickerbocker Magazine*, the *Virginian* and *The Southern Literary Messenger*.

COOPER, James Fenimore 1789-1851 - Novelist. His second novel, *The Spy* (1821), set during the Revolutionary War, brought him fame and wealth. *The Pioneers* (1823) introduced Natty Bumppo, who then appeared in subsequent "Leatherstocking Tales": *The Last of the Mohicans* (1826), *The Prairie* (1827), *The Pathfinder* (1840) and *The Deerslayer* (1841). These made him popular in Europe. He also wrote a series of sea novels, starting with *The Pilot* (1823), and a *History of the Navy of the United States of America* (1839).

DANA, Richard Henry 1787-1889 - Though not so well known today as his son (who wrote *Two Years Before the Mast*), Dana, Sr. once had a sold reputation as a poet. He also loved and wrote about the sea, though from the shore, where his poor health as a boy often sent him. One of his major poems was "The Buccaneer", about a murder by a pirate. He was briefly a lawyer and a member of the legislature, before ill-health pushed him to literary pursuits, first in assisting Channing with the *North American Review*. He published his first poem, "The Dying Raven", in 1825 and his first collection, *Poems and Prose Writings*, in 1833. Rufus Wilmot Griswold said of him (perhaps too optimistically), "All the writings of Dana belong to the permanent literature of the country".

DAWES, Rufus 1803-1859 - A Massachusetts poet. His major works include *The Valley of the Nashaway and other Poems*, *Athenia of Damascus*, *Geraldine* (a long narrative poem), and *Nix's Mate: An Historical Romance of America* (1839) Poe wrote other unflattering remarks about him, quoting Griswold, in *Poets and Poetry of America* : "As a poet the standing of Mr. Dawes is as yet unsettled; there being a wide difference of opinion respecting his writings."

DOANE, Bishop George Washington 1799-1859 - Bishop, orator and educator. While at Hartford as professor at Washington (later Trinity) College in 1824, he edited the *Episcopal Watchman*. He became rector of Trinity Church in 1830 and bishop of New Jersey in 1832. Financial problems growing from his efforts in founding two schools led to a trial in which he was cleared. He published poetry (*Songs by the Way*, 1824) and speeches. His son

edited his *Life and Writings* (1861).

DOW, Jesse Erskine 1809-1850 - A journalist and poet. Having served on the Constitution from 1835 to 1836, he later wrote *Sketches From the Logs of Old Ironsides* (1839) about the experience. He, Poe and F. W. Thomas met in 1840 and shared interests in cryptography, politics and literature. He ended his days in Washington D. C.

DOWNING, Jack - This signature appears to be something of an 'in' joke: Downing was a fictional character created by Seba Smith.

DU SOLLE, John Stephenson 1810-1876 - "Colonel" John Stephenson Du Solle was the editor of *Spirit of the Times*, a penny paper which attacked various wealthy interests. His offices were across from those of *Graham's*. A friend of Poe's, he seems to have had a sulphurous reputation. He later settled in New York, where he became private secretary to P. T. Barnum.

EARLE, Pliny 1809-1892 – A Massachusetts physician (and minor poet) who specialized in working with the insane. He was the first to give non-religious lectures in asylums and pioneered education and entertainment as part of the treatment there. A number of his writings were collected as *The Curability of Insanity; a Series of Studies* (1887). He helped found a number of medical organizations including the American Medical Association. In addition to works such as *A Visit to Thirteen Asylums for the Insane in Europe* (1840); *The History, Description, and Statistics of the Bloomingdale Asylum* (1848) and *Institutions for the Insane in Prussia, Germany, and Austria* (1853), he published *Marathon and other Poems* (1841).

EMBURY, Emma Catherine 1806-1863 - She contributed to a number of periodicals, often as 'Ian the', and published volumes such as *The Blind Girl and Other Tales*, *Nature's Gems, or American Wild Flowers* and *The Waldorf Family, a Grandfather's Legend*, and was well-known in her time. Her literary salon included Poe, Rufus Griswold and others.

EMERSON, Ralph Waldo 1803-1882 – Poet and essayist. Briefly a minister. Though known as the "Sage of Concord", the central figure in Transcendentalism, he refused to be bound by that philosophy. Despite many advanced ideas, he lived an orderly New Englander's life. He was an eloquent and musical speaker, popular even as he questioned accepted ideas on religion and other subjects. His works include: *Essays (First Series)* (1841); *Essays (Second Series)* (1844); *Representative Men* (1850);

A Biographical Dictionary of Poe's Subjects

English Traits (1856); *The Conduct of Life* (1860); *Society and Solitude* (1870); *Letters and Social Aims* (1876), and two volumes of verse.

EVERETT Edward 1794-1865 – A clergyman who had a long political career, serving as Congressman, governor and ambassador. He was also Harvard's first professor of Greek. His speeches were published as *Orations and Speeches on Various Occasions* (1853-68). He gave the principal address at Gettysburg, only to have its two hours eclipsed by the two minutes of Lincoln's speech.

FAY, Theodore Sedgwiek 1807-1898 – Poet, novelist and journalist. Associate editor of the New York *Mirror* and later secretary of the American legation in Berlin (1837-1853), then minister resident in Bern (1853-1861). He wrote books of history and geography as well poems and a romance. but was most known for the novel *Norman Leslie*, which the young Poe savaged in a review in the *Messenger* (1835), antagonizing the writer's influential friends.

FRENCH, James S. 1807-86 - Poe doubtfully credits him with writing a life of David Crockett which Crockett himself disliked enough to write his own Narrative as a response. His *Elkswatawa or the Prophet of the West* (1836) was about General William Henry Harrison's campaign against the Shawnee chief Tecumseh and seems to mix genuine sympathy for the native population with the melodrama then popular.

FROST, John 1800-1859 - A principal and then a teacher in Boston and Philadelphia, he resigned in 1845 to compile histories and biographies, ultimately publishing over 300, including *History of the World* (3 vols.); *Pictorial History of the United States* (1844); *Beauties of English History*, *Wild Scenes of a Hunter's Life*, *Illustrious Mechanics*, *Book of Heroes*, *Book of the Army*, and *Book of the Navy*.

GALLAGHER, William Davis 1808-1894 - Journalist and poet. He edited a number of Ohio publications, while gaining attention for his prose tales and poems from about 1828 on. Despite two stints in Washington, D.C., he ultimately took up agriculture and moved to Kentucky. "The Wreck of the Hornet" was his first widely popular poem. He also wrote on agriculture in Ohio and on the Civil War.

GODEY, Louis Antoine 1804-1878 - He moved to Philadelphia from New York and, in 1830, founded the very successful *Godey's Lady's Book* and ran it until he sold it to a stock company in 1877. Having also published the *Daily Chronicle* newspaper,

Jarvis' Musical Library and *Young People's Book*, he left a fortune of over $1,000,000.

GOULD, Hannah Flagg 1789-1865 - A New England poet who lived with her father and published a great deal for magazines, in part, apparently from financial need. Her *Poems* (1832 was widely popular and often reprinted. She wrote a great deal for children, as well as religious, patriotic and abolitionist works. In 1826, she wrote a poem about Maelzel's chess-playing automaton in the *Saturday Evening Gazette* - this appears to be the first document by an American woman about chess. Her religious poem "A Name In the Sand" is still widely quoted.

GRAHAM, George Rex 1813-1894 - A lawyer and editor of the *Saturday Evening Post*, he then published *Graham's Magazine*, in which the current work was published. Poe was hired as book review editor in February 1841, then resigned in April 1842 and was replaced by Rufus W. Griswold. After buying the *North American* in 1846, Graham lost a great deal of money in the market and with it both magazines.

GREELEY, Horace 1811-1872 - After several other ventures, in 1834 Greeley and a partner published the *New Yorker*, a weekly which lasted seven years and brought him to prominence. He founded the Tribune, a daily, in 1841, and became as well-known as his very successful paper. In the Fifties, he became a dedicated opponent of slavery. His advocacy of homesteading led him to his famous quote "Go West, young man". He later ran unsuccessfully for president.

HALE, Sarah Josepha 1788-1879 – Writer. the first female editor of a magazine and – author of "Mary Had a Little Lamb" (1830). A widow, she began writing (1822) to support her family. She edited the *Ladies' Magazine* from 1828 until Godey bought it in 1837. As *Godey's Lady's Book*, it became the major woman's magazine of its time. She collected women's poetry in *The Ladies Wreath* (1837). Her *Woman's Record; or, Sketches of All Distinguished Women, From "The Beginning Till A.D. 1850"* (1853) includes 2,500 biographical entries.

HALLECK, Fitz-Greene 1790-1867 – Poet and satirist. With Joseph Rodman Drake, he wrote "the Croaker Papers" (1819), which appeared in the *New York Evening Post*. He satirized Byron in *Fanny* (1819). His elegy to Drake, "Green Be the Turf above Thee", and the recital piece "Marco Bozzaris" are two of his popular pieces. He was also secretary to John Jacob Astor.

HAWKS, Francis Lister 1798-1866 - A Southern clergyman and orator who began as a lawyer, he became a deacon in 1827, then a priest in the Episcopalian Church. As historiographer of the church, he produced two of eighteen planned volumes of a history of the Church of England in America but abandoned the task after these were criticized. In 1837, he co-founded the quarterly *New York Review*. Financial troubles connected with St. Thomas' Hall, a school he founded (1839), so damaged his reputation that in 1844 he refused a bishopric. Besides church history, he wrote other histories and biographies.

HEATH, James E. 1792-1862 - A Virginian lawyer who, as first editor of the *Southern Literary Messenger*, encouraged Southern writers to break free of Northern models. In commenting on Poe's "Fall of the House of Usher", he suggested that Dickens had dealt a death blow to such "wild, improbable and terrible tales".

HENRY, Caleb Sprague 1804-1884 - Journalist and minister in several different denominations. He established the *American Advocate of Peace*, the organ of the American Peace Society (1834). In 1834, he co-founded the *New York Review*. While rector of New York's St. Clement's from 1847 to 1850, edited *The Churchman* and was briefly political editor of the *New York Times*. He wrote several histories, essays, and lectures.

HERBERT, Henry William 1807-1858 - A prolific author despite numerous misfortunes, he was born in England, but came to America in 1830 and taught the classics. He founded the *American Monthly Magazine*, but later made Charles Fenno Hoffman editor. His anonymous first novel, *The Brothers, a Tale of the Fronde* (1834), was very successful. From 1837 to 1855, he published numerous others. He was the first sportswriter in America, writing as "Frank Forester" for sporting papers. His second wife left him after three months, announcing this in the papers. In response he held a grand dinner for old friends - only one of whom came. When the dinner was done, he walked to a full-length mirror, took aim and shot himself through the heart.

HOFFMAN, Charles Fenno 1806-1884 - Having briefly practiced law, he became the first editor of the *Knickerbocker Magazine* (1833). Later connected with the *American Monthly Magazine*, which serialized his novel *Vanderlyn* in 1837, and with the *New York Mirror*. His poetry was first collected in *The Vigil of Faith and Other Poems* (1842).

HOFFMAN, David 1784-1854 - Maryland lawyer who wrote extensively on the law. He also wrote *Miscellaneous Thoughts on Men, Manners, and Things* by "Anthony Grumbler, of Grumbleton Hall, Esq."(1837); *Viator, or a Peep into my Note-Book* (1841) and two volumes of a history of the world called *Chronicles selected from the Originals of Cartaphilus, the Wandering Jew*.

HOLDEN, Ezra 1803-1846 - Little information is available on this journalist, editor from 1803 to 1846 of Philadelphia's *Saturday Courier*, which had a wide circulation. In 1839, he reviewed Poe's *Tales of the Grotesque and Arabesque* in that paper.

HOLMES, Dr. Oliver Wendell 1809-1894 – Physician and humorist, father of the Supreme Court Justice. His poem on the "Constitution" helped save that ship. He is most known as the author of *Autocrat of the Breakfast Table*, which first appeared as pieces in the *Atlantic Monthly*, which he founded with Lowell (1857). This was followed by the *Professor at the Breakfast Table* (1859) and other works. At Boston's Saturday Club he met Emerson, Longfellow, Whittier, Lowell, and other major figures and was considered the best talker among them.

INGRAHAM, Joseph Holt 1809-1860 - Clergyman who'd also been to sea, served in a South American revolution and started to write before he was twenty. He published *The Southwest, by a Yankee* (1836) and a series of adventure tales, before taking orders in 1855. He then published religious romances such as *The Prince of the House of David, or Three Years in the Holy City* (1855} and *The Pillar of Fire, or Israel in Bondage* (1859).

IRVING, Washington 1783 - 1859 - New Yorker Washington Irving is still best known today for "Rip Van Winkel" and "The Legend of Sleep Hollow". He also wrote a good deal of travel writing and a biography of George Washington. The first American writer to be well received in Europe. Poe, having met him in 1837, found him over-rated, but may have envied his wealth and popularity.

JONES, John Beauchamp 1810-1866 - A journalist, he established the *Southern Monitor (1857)*, supporting Southern interests. His works include *Books of Visions* (1847); *Rural Sports, a Poem* (1848), *The Western Merchant* (1848), *Wild Western Scenes* (1849), *The Rival Belles* (1852), *Life and Adventures of a Country Merchant* (1854), *Freaks of Fortune* (1854), and a *Rebel War Clerk's Diary at the Confederate States Capital* (1866).

A Biographical Dictionary of Poe's Subjects

KENNEDY, John P 1795-1870 - Author and politician. In 1852, he became Secretary of the Navy and was instrumental in Commander Perry's success in Japan. He wrote part of Thackeray's *The Virginians*. His own works include satire, speeches, reports, and the novels *Swallow Barn*, about rural life in Virginia (1832); *Horse-Shoe Robinson, a Tale of the Tory Ascendency* (1835): and *Rob of the Bowl, a Legend of St. Inigoes (1838)*, about Maryland in the days of the second Lord Baltimore.

LANGTREE, Samuel D. - Little is known about this Washington D. C. publisher, whose *American Pamphlets* (1839?) is considered an important resource on the nineteenth century. The material, from the late eighteenth century to 1838 covers topics as different as government, travel, religion, slavery, agriculture and more. The law firm he ran with a Mr. O'Sullivan from 1837 to the late 1840's was at one point the official printer for the United States government. They also published the *United States Magazine* and *Democratic Review*. He also briefly served as editor of New York's *Knickerbocker*.

LEGARE, Hugh Swinton 1789-1843 - A South Carolina statesman (who pronounced his last name 'leh-gree'), he held a number of offices, He helped publish the *Southern Review* and later wrote on law and democracy for the *New York Review*. As attorney-general under President Tyler, he died while accompanying him to the unveiling of the Bunker Hill monument.

LESLIE, Eliza 1787-1858 – Her father was a personal friend of Ben Franklin's. She wrote poetry, only starting to write prose – a cookbook – at 40. She then edited the popular annual *The Gift*, and wrote very popular books on cookery and housekeeping, including the *Domestic Cookery Book* (1837), *Ladies' Receipt Book* (1848) and the *Behavior Book* (1853).

LIEBER, Francis 1800-1872 - Born in Germany, he had a variety of adventures in Europe before coming to America in 1872. He became a professor of history and political economy at the University of South Carolina, Columbia, until 1856, when he went to Columbia College, New York. His inaugural address on "Individualism; and Socialism, or Communism" was published by the college. He wrote against secession (while in South Carolina) and later for the Union. He also wrote *Guerrilla Parties considered with reference to the Law and Usages of War*, and *Instructions for the Government of the Armies of the United States in the Field* (1863)

as well as a number of other works on law and the penal system.

LOCKE, Richard Adams 1800-1871 - Editor of the *New York Sun* and *The New Era*, he was responsible for two hoaxes. The first, known as the "Moon Hoax", (1835) purported among other things to describe the inhabitants of the moon. Even some scientific men were taken in by this, and it was reprinted as a pamphlet in 1871. The other was *The Lost Manuscript of Mungo Park*. Towards the end of his life he left journalism because of ill-health and was appointed to the New York Custom House.

LONGFELLOW, Henry Wadsworth 1807-1882 – Still one of the most popular American poets. Head of Harvard's modern language program for 18 years. His poems "The Wreck of the Hesperus"(1841), *Evangeline* (1847), *Hiawatha* (1855) and "Paul Revere's Ride"(1863) were immensely popular and remain famous today. Other works include *Hyperion* (1839) and *Christus: A Mystery* (1872), and a translation of Dante's *Divine Comedy* (1865-67). In 1841 he wrote to Poe, "...you are destined to stand among the first romance-writers of the country."

LOUD, Marguerite St. Leon c.1800-1889 - A Philadelphia poet, she contributed to magazines such the *United States Gazette* and published *Wayside Flowers* (1851). Griswold included her work in *Female Poets of America*. Her husband offered Poe $100 to edit one of her books.

LOWELL, James Russell 1819-1891 - The celebrated New England poet was still young when Poe wrote the current work, but already friends with Emerson and other Transcendentalists. In 1848, he was corresponding editor for *The Anti-Slavery Standard*, where he also published poems from 1843 to 1846. But it was in the *Boston Courier* that he began to publish the "Biglow Papers" beginning in 1846 and ending in 1848. These satirical poems in Yankee dialect were soon considered classics. While continuing purely literary endeavors such as *Conversations with Some of the Old Poets* (1845) and "The Vision of Sir Launfal" (1845), he wrote for the *Dial*, the *Democratic Review*, the *Massachusetts Quarterly Review* and *Putnam's Monthly*. He succeeded Longfellow as professor of modern languages at Harvard and also served as a diplomat in Spain and England. When he met Poe (in 1845), Poe had a hangover. He later said of Poe, "Three-fifths of him genius and two-fifths sheer fudge."

LUNT, George 1803-1885 - A Massachusetts lawyer, he was for a while editor of the Boston

Courier around the time of the Civil War. He was active as a public speaker, first as a Whig and then as a Democrat. He wrote several books of poems, including *Poems* (1839) and *The Union, a Poem* (1860), and books on New England.

MATHEWS, Cornelius 1817-1889 - In 1850, the *Prompter* described him as a "prolific" novelist and editor. The *Southern Quarterly Review*, in reviewing his collected works, said, "Mathews... is still, we understand, a very young man; yet here... He appears before us as critic and novelist; poet and dramatist; politician and essayist." His works include *Behemoth, or the mound-builders*, *Wakondah, the master of life*, *Moneypenny or, the Heart of the World*, and *The Politicians, a comedy* and a book on *International Copyright*.

McHENRY, James 1785-1845 – Merchant, poet, novelist, editor and doctor, born Irish. In 1824 he edited Philadelphia's *American Monthly Magazine*, for which he wrote "O'Halloran, or the Insurgent, a Romance of the Irish Rebellion". Some other works were *The Wilderness, or Braddock's Times, a Tale of the West* (1823); *A Spectre of the Forest, or Annals of the Housatonic* (1823); and *The Hearts of Steel, an Irish Historical Tale of the Last Century* (1825). His poetry includes *Waltham, an American Revolutionary Tale, in Three Cantos* (1823) and *The Usurper, an Historical Tragedy, in Five Acts*, a successful play. A friend of Andrew Jackson, he published "Jackson's Wreath," a poem (1829), in tribute to him.

MCJILTON, John Nelson 1805-1875 . Minister and poet. Little remains of his work today. Two works, both from 1846, which may be typical are *Washington: the model of character for American youth*: an address delivered to the boys of the Baltimore public school and "Day of Freedom" set to music by J.M. Deems. Though white, he was the pastor of two black churches, from at least 1843 to 1845. His name is on one of the Washington Memorial Stones as a Maryland Mason from the Grand Lodge of ancient Free and Accepted Masons of Maryland 1850. Poe suspected him in 1841 of being the author of a pseudonymous coded letter. McJilton denied this. He contributed to the *Southern Literary Messenger* while Poe was editor.

McMICHAEL Morton 1807-1879 - A journalist, he also served as alderman, sheriff and mayor in Philadelphia. In 1826 he became editor of the *Saturday Evening Post*. He later became sole proprietor of the *North American and United States Gazette* (1854) until his death

MELLEN, Grenville 1799-1841 – Poet. Son of a chief justice of the Supreme Court of Maine. He published poems in various periodicals and edited the *Portland Advertiser* and the *Monthly Miscellany*. He wrote of the young America: "Ours is the land and age of gold/ And ours the hallow'd time!"

MITCHELL, John Kearsley 1798-1858 - A physician who traveled three times to the East as ship's surgeon, he settled in Philadelphia and taught successively at the Philadelphia Medical Institute and then Jefferson Medical College, while continuing to practice. In addition to poetry and a book *On the Wisdom, Goodness, and Power of God as illustrated in the Properties of Water* (1834), he anticipated more modern ideas on disease in *On the Cryptogamous Origin of Malarious and Epidemic Fevers* (1849).

MORRIS, George 1802-1864 - At 15, he was already writing for the *New York Gazette* and the *American*. In 1823 he co-founded the *New York Mirror* with Samuel Woodworth. Having served in the New York militia, he was generally addressed as General Morris. He wrote prose and verse works, but was most known as a song-writer, whose lyrics sold well for more than 20 years. Some popular ones were "Near the Lake where drooped the Willow," "We were Boys together," "My Mother's Bible," "Whip-poor-Will," and "Woodman, Spare That Tree," which was quoted during a debate in the House of Commons.

MORRIS, Robert 1809-1874 - Editor of the daily *Philadelphia Inquirer*. He may have been that paper's anonymous reviewer of Poe's "Prose Romances".

NEAL, John 1793-1876 – Poet, novelist and journalist. Once very popular for such novels as *Keep Cool* (1817), *Logan* (1827) and *Randolph* (1823). He moved to England in 1824 and wrote for British journals, among them *Blackwood's Magazine*. After settling in Maine (1827), he wrote more stories, articles, novels, and an autobiography, *Wandering Recollections of a Somewhat Busy Life* (1869).

NICHOLS, Rebecca Shepherd Reed 1819-1903 - In Kentucky, she edited the *Pennant*, a daily, with her husband. When they moved to Cincinnati (1836), she edited *The Guest*, a literary journal. First published as "Ellen", she was best known for a series of letters she wrote to the *Cincinnatti Herald* as "Kate Cleaveland". She also wrote *Bernice, and other Poems* (1844) and *Songs of the Heart* (1852).

A Biographical Dictionary of Poe's Subjects

O'NEAL, Joseph Clay - A humorist, he edited the *Pennsylvanian* (1831-44) and began a series of character sketches there called the "City Worthies". Later collected in *Charcoal Sketches* (1837), these were republished in London under the patronage of Charles Dickens. He also established the *Saturday Gazette*, a successful, largely humorous periodical.

OTIS, James Frederick 1808-1867 - A lawyer who became a journalist and an ardent abolitionist. In 1836 he wrote for Washington's very influential *Daily National Intelligencer*, the capital city's most influential newspaper. He also contributed to the *Southern Literary Messenger* when Poe was editing

PALFREY, John Gorham 1796-1881 - A Unitarian clergyman, historian, and proprietor and editor of the *North American Review* (1835-43) and member of the House of Representatives (1847-49). He wrote a major *History of New England* (1858-75). In a review in the *North American Review* for April, 1821, he pointed out that early American history might be material for fiction, prompting Lydia Maria Child, then Miss Francis, to write the popular novel *Hobomok: a Tale of Early Times. By an American*.

PAULDING, James Kirke 1778-1860 – [NOTE: The signature differs from another sample and might be that of Hiram Paulding, a military man who wrote *Journal of A Cruise of the U. S. Schooner Dolphin*,. But James Kirke, known to Poe, is the most likely subject.] With Washington Irving and his brother he founded the New York Periodical *Salmagundi*. He wrote a number of satires, including *The Diverting History of John Bull and Brother Jonathan* (1812) and the *Lay of the Scottish Fiddle* (1813).

PEABODY, William B. O. 1799-1848 - Teacher, lawyer, politician and Unitarian minister who wrote several well-regarded poems, he was also this country's first editor of Shakespeare.

PIERPONT, Rev. John 1785-1866 - A poet, lawyer and merchant in Boston, then Baltimore. In 1816, he became a pastor. His strong pro-temperance and anti-slavery opinions led him into conflict with his first congregation but also, briefly, into politics. A scholar and a public speaker, he published *Airs of Palestine*, a book of poems (1816). His poem "Warren's Address at the Battle of Bunker Hill" was one of his most well-known. He was also a friend of Bryant's.

PIKE, Albert 1809-91- A New Englander, in 1831 he began to explore the West, starting in Ohio, and ultimately ended up in Arkansas, where he taught and became editor of the *Arkansas Advocate* in 1833. His "Hymns to the Gods", published in

Blackwood's Magazine in 1839, first made him famous as a poet. He also became known as a lawyer, then fought in the Mexican and Civil Wars (in the latter as a Confederate). Besides *Prose Sketches and Poems* (1834) and *Reports of Cases in the Supreme Court of Arkansas* (1840-'5), he wrote on freemasonry.

REYNOLDS, Jeremiah N. ?1799-1858? - Poe's "The Narrative of Arthur Gordon Pym of Nantucket" (1837) is based on Reynold's actual travels on a whaler. Poe reviewed his *Address, on the Subject of a Surveying and Exploring Expedition to the Pacific Ocean and South Seas* (1836) in the *Southern Literary Messenger*. He also seems to be the same (obscure) man whose article on a white whale named 'Mocha Dick' in the *Knickerbocker* magazine (May 1839) inspired the name for "Moby Dick".

SANDERSON, John 1783-1844 - Having started to study law, he became a teacher, ultimately a professor of Latin and Greek in the Philadelphia high school. He wrote a number of non-fiction works, including (with his brother) two volumes of the *Biography of the Signers of the Declaration of Independence* (1820), a pamphlet opposing the plan to exclude classical languages from Girard College (1826), *Sketches of Paris* (1838) and portions of *The American in London*, which appeared in the *Knickerbocker Magazine*.

SARGENT, Epes 1813-1880 - A poet and a playwright who also wrote *The Standard Speller; Containing Exercises for Oral Spelling and Sentences for Silent Spelling by Writing from Dictation In Which the Representative Words and the Anomalous Words of the English Language are so Classified as to Indicate Their Pronunciation, and to be Fixed in the Memory by Association*.

SEDGWICK, Catherine Maria 1789-1867 – A popular novelist whose subjects included Native Americans and women's issues. Her first novel *A New-England Tale; or, Sketches of New-England Character and Manners* (1822) grew out of her conversion to Unitarianism and ideas on religious tolerance. *Redwood* (1824) was her second. Her third, *Hope Leslie* (1827) made her America's most famous woman novelist. A later novel, *Married or Single?* (1857) argued for a woman's independence. Some of her many short stories were collected in *Tales and Sketches* (1835), *Stories for Young Persons* (1841), and *Tales of City Life* (1850).

SIGOURNEY, Lydia Huntley 1791-1865 - A precocious child, she had a genteel education, and taught young women before publishing *Moral Pieces in Prose and Verse* (1815). After marrying a Hartford merchant, she continued to write, at first for pleasure, then for income after her husband lost his fortune. She became a popular and prolific writer, who wrote over forty books as well as a number of articles. Her somewhat sentimental poetry was so popular on the Continent that the Queen of France gave her a diamond bracelet. Among her works are: "Traits of the Aborigines of America," a poem (1822); *Sketch of Connecticut Forty Years Since* (1824); *Letters to Young Ladies* (which went through 20 editions from 1833 through 1853); the pro-temperance *Water-Drops*, (1847); Letters to My Pupils (1850); "The Faded Hope," in memory of her son who died at nineteen (1852); and *The Man of Uz, and other Poems* (1862).

SIMMS, W. Gilmore 1806-1870 - Was already writing at seven. *Lyricla and other poems* (1827) was his first public attempt at literature (1827). His involvement with the *Charlestown City Gazette* which (in South Carolina) took the Union side in a controversy ruined him and in 1833 he devoted himself to literature. Though he wrote more poetry, he was most known as a writer of fiction, largely about the South, "The Yemassee" being his best-known novel. Poe called him America's best novelist after Cooper, but he is not generally so well-regarded.

SLIDELL (MACKENZIE), Alexander 1803-1848 - (Mackenzie, his mother's name, was a later addition.) An author, he was at least well-known as a naval officer, who served in the Mediterranean, the West Indies, near Brazil and in the Pacific. While on the brig "Somers" in 1842, he discovered plans for a mutiny and three seamen were executed. His conduct was subsequently approved, but the young men in question were of good family and the aftermath shadowed his life. His first book, *A Year in Spain, by a Young American* (1829), was immediately popular in America and in England. He also wrote *Popular Essays on Naval Subjects* (1833); *The American in England* (1835); *Spain Revisited* (1836); and several biographies of naval figures.

SMITH, Seba 1792-1868 – Though he edited several New England periodicals, his most famous production was a series of satirical letters under the pen-name of "Major Jack Downing". These very popular pieces were published in a collection in 1833. His other works include the verse romance *Powhatan* (1841), *New Elements of Geometry*

(1850) and *Way Down East, or Portraitures of Yankee Life* (1855).

SMITH, Richard Penn 1790-1854 - Lawyer, novelist dramatist, poet. From 1822-1827 he edited the *Aurora*. His first novel, *The Forsaken* (1831), concerns the American Revolution. He also wrote two volumes of short stories, entitled *The Actress of Padua and other Tales*, and many plays, including *Caius Marius*, *William Penn*, and *The Water Witch*. His plays were often produced and Smith helped develop a national American theater. He was also the anonymous author of *Col. Crockett's Exploits and Adventures in Texas*, a hoax which helped mythologize Crockett.

SPARKS, Jared 1789-1866 - Minister, historian and professor at Harvard, he wrote a number of religious works and biographies, but above all collected the papers of George Washington and, with the authorization of Congress, *The Diplomatic Correspondence of the American Revolution* (1829-30). He was also. the originator and first editor of the *American Almanac and Repository of Useful Knowledge* (1830-'61).

SPRAGUE, Charles 1791-1875 - Yet another son of one of the participants in the Boston Tea Party, he was a banker and poet, well-known for his theatrical prologues, but also wrote for domestic pieces such as "The Brothers", "I see Thee Still", and "The Family Meeting"." His work was collected in *Prose and Poetical Writings, revised by the Author* (1850).

STEDMAN, Elizabeth Clementine 1810-1889 - Essayist and poet. Contributed to numerous magazines, one of them, the *Newark Daily Advertiser*, edited by her second husband. Her poems have been collected in *Poems* (1867), *Felicita* (1855) and *Bianca Cappella* (1873). Her more famous son, Edmund Clarence Stedman, wrote one of the best essays on Poe and edited a standard edition of his work.

STEPHENS, Anne S. 1813-1886 - A New England author, she founded the *Portland Magazine* in 1835 and in 1836 published *The Portland Sketchbook*, a collection of local writing. Moving with her husband to New York in 1837, she edited *The Ladies' Companion* and wrote for *Graham's Magazine* and *Peterson's Magazine*, then founded *The Ladies' World* (1843) and *The Illustrated New Monthly* (1846). Her poem "The Polish Boy" was long a favorite. She also wrote several short stories. Her first long novel, *Fashion and Famine* (1854), went through several editions in France. She was admired for realistic if "intense" writing and did research in hospitals, institutions, etc.. Her other works include *Zana, or the Heiress of Clare Hall* (1854), *The Old Homestead* (1855), *Sybil Chase* (1862) and *Ahmo's Plot* (1863) as well as a *Pictorial History of the War for the Union.*

STOCKTON, Thomas Hewlings 1808-1868 - A doctor who became a clergyman, he was an abolitionist and a reformer. He left Baltimore for Philadelphia because of restrictions on the discussion of slavery. He served as chaplain to the United States House of Representatives (1833-5; 1859-62). He edited the *Christian World* and the *Bible Times*, and published a number of books derived from the Bible or on Christian subjects, as well as a ballad, "Stand Up for Jesus" (1858), and a number of other poems.

STONE, Colonel William Leete 1792-1844 - Raised in what were then the 'wilds' of New York State, he later used the experience in his fiction. He was editor of a number of upstate and Connecticut papers and helped edit *The Knights of the Round Table*, a Hartford literary journal. He was active in a number of causes, including Abolitionism and supporting Greek independence. He was successfully sued by James Fenimore Cooper for two reviews, to the dismay of those who felt this threatened the liberty of the press. Among his many works are several on New York State and Wyoming history, *Tales and Sketches* (1834), derived from native and Revolutionary sources and *Border Wars of the American Revoluton* (1837).

STORY, Joseph 1779-1845 – He served in Congress and the Massachusetts Legislature before becoming a Federal circuit judge and then serving on the Massachusetts Supreme Court (but several times refusing to become Chief Justice). He wrote more textbooks on jurisprudence than any other writer of his time, including *Commentaries on the Law of Bailments* (1832), *Commentaries on the Constitution of the United States* (1833), *Commentaries on the Conflict of Laws* (1834) and *Commentaries on Equity Jurisprudence* (1835-'6).

STREET, Alfred B. 1811-1881 - A New York lawyer who edited the *Northern Light* (1843-1844) and became state librarian (1845). He was also successful as a poet with works such as *The Burning of Schenectady, and other Poems* (1842), *Fugitive Poems* (1846) and *Frontenac, or the Atotarho of the Iroquois, a Metrical Romance* (1849). He produced histories and other factual works as

well, including *The Council of Revision of the State of New York* (1859), *A Digest of Taxation in the United States* (1863) and *The Indian Pass*, about explorations in Essex county, New York (1869).

THOMAS, Frederick W. 1811-1866 - A lawyer, minister, professor, writer and editor. His poem "The Emigrant" (1832) once was widely published in periodicals and school books. He wrote the popular novel *Clinton Bradshaw* (1835), as well as the less successful *East and West* (1836) and *Howard Pinckney* (1837). His numerous poems and sketches are included in *John Randolph of Roanoke, and other Public Characters* (1853). He met Poe in 1840 and they corresponded frequently after that. In the *Poets of America*, Rufus Wilmot Griswold said: "He has a nice discrimination of the peculiarities of character, which give light and shade to the surface of society, and a hearty relish for that peculiar humor which abounds in that portion of our country which undoubtedly embraces most that is original and striking in manners and unrestrained in conduct. He must rank with the first illustrators of manners in the Valley of the Mississippi."

THOMSON, Charles West 1798-1879 - A poet and Episcopalian minister, he wrote *The Limner* (1822), a book of prose sketches, *The Phantom Barge, and other Poems* (1822) and a number of other poems, as well as articles for periodicals.

TUCKER, Judge Nathaniel Beverly 1784-1851 - A Virginian lawyer and later professor of law at William and Mary, he wrote several political novels. He published his first novel, *George Balcombe*, anonymously, though it received favorable reviews, Poe's among them. His prediction of Dickens' success may have been one of the most memorable points of his career. He corresponded with Poe when he was editor of the *Southern Literary Messenger.*

TUCKERMAN, Henry T. 1813-1871 - An art historian, critic and literary figure from a wealthy Massachusetts family, he was a friend of Herman Melville's and a founding member of the Century Association, one of the oldest Fifth Avenue clubs. He wrote numerous pieces for *Putnam's Monthly*, *Harper's New Monthly*, *Scribner's Monthly* and other periodicals.

WALSH, Robert 1784-1859 – Deafness ended his career in law. In 1810, he wrote a "Letter on the Genius and Disposition of the French Government" which became very popular in England. He founded (1811) *The American Review of History and Politics,* the first quarterly in the United States. From 1819 to 1839 he was connected to the *National Gazette*, which he founded. During the same time he also worked on the *Magazine of Foreign Literature* and the *American Review*. He also wrote a number of biographical sketches and other factual works. After moving to Paris in 1836, he was consul from 1845-1851 and ended his days in that city.

WARE, Henry 1794-1843 – A Massachusetts clergyman who edited the Unitarian organ *The Christian Examiner* (1819 – 1822). He published *Hints on Extemporaneous Preaching* (1824), *Sermons on the Offices and Character of Jesus Christ* (1825), *The Formation of Christian Character* (1831) and *The Life of the Saviour* (1832), as well as various memoirs, sermons, essays, and poems.

WETMORE, Prosper Montgomery 1798-1876. - A military man, merchant and lobbyist who also wrote poetry, he was one of the founders of the American Art Union, where he was president from 1847 to 1849. He was also co-editor of the *New York Courier and Enquirer* when it was established in 1829.

WHITTIER John Greenleaf 1807-1892 – New England poet, novelist, and journalist. Also a devout Quaker and a fervent abolitionist., long associated with the abolitionist William Lloyd Garrison. He worked with several publications, including the *New England Weekly* (1830) and, from its founding (1857), the *Atlantic Monthly*. *Legends of New England* (1831) was his first book of poems. He published several others, including *Snowbound* (1866), which included his best-known poem of the same name. His prose works include *The Stranger in Lowell* (1845), *Supernaturalism in New England* (1847), and *Leaves from Margaret Smith's Journal* (1849).

WILD, Horatio Hastings 1811-1888 - A Northeastern journalist and minister, ordained in 1845. Among his works were *Corrected Proofs* (1837) a volume of sketches, a *Life of Christ* (1850) and *Sacred Poetical Quotations* (1851). He also edited books of scenes from the Scriptures, as well

as *Benjamin Franklin's Autobiography, with a Narrative of his Public Life and Services* (1849).

WILDE, Richard Henry 1789-1847 - Born in Ireland, he was a lawyer, then congressman from Georgia, before moving to Europe. In 1843 he became professor of law at the University of Louisiana. The only work he published himself was *Conjectures and Researches concerning the Love, Madness, and Imprisonment of Torquato Tasso* (1842). His lyric "The Lament of the Captive", published in 1815 without his authorization, became very popular as "My Life is like the Summer Rose" and was both set to music and presented (falsely) as a translation from the Greek.

WILLIS, Nathaniel Parker 1806-1867 - Poet, novelist and journalist. He founded *The American Monthly Magazine* (1829-31) which then merged with the *New York Mirror*. In 1831 he became foreign correspondent from Europe and Asia Minor He later helped found the *New Mirror* which became the more successful *New York Home Journal*. He wrote popular versions of scripture such as "Absalom" and "The Leper". His secular pieces, "The Belfry Pigeon," "Unseen Spirits,"and "Parrhasius the Painter" were widely anthologized. However, long poems like "Melanie"(1835) and "The Lady Jane"(1844) and his novel *Paul Fane* (1857) were less successful, as were the plays *Bianca Visconti* (1839) and *Tortesa, the Usurer* (1839). He also wrote short stories and travel pieces. He was one of the most widely read American authors in his lifetime. A good friend of Poe's, he employed him several times and first published "The Raven" (1845).

WILMER, Lambert A. 1805-1863 - An author and journalist, he edited the Baltimore Saturday Visitor and was connected with the Pennsylvanian. He wrote a *New System of Grammar, The Quacks of Helicon* (1851), *Life, Travels, and Adventures of Ferdinand de Soto* (1858); and *Our Press-Gang, or a Complete Exposition of the Corruptions and Crimes of the American Newspapers* (1859).

SOURCES

Web sites are grouped after printed sources.
All sites were accessed December 2004.

On Poe

Allen, Hervey. *Israfel, the life and times of Edgar Allan Poe*. New York: Farrar & Rinehart, 1934.

Chivers, Thomas Holly, *Chivers' Life of Poe*, ed. Richard Beale Davis, New York: E. P Dutton and Co. Inc., 1952.

Hayes, Kevin J., ed. *The Cambridge Companion to Edgar Allan Poe (Cambridge Companions to Literature)*. Cambridge: Cambridge University Press, 2002.

Jacobs, Robert D., *The Courage of a Critic: Edgar Poe as Editor*. Baltimore: The Edgar Allan Poe Society of Baltimore, 1971.

Kennedy, J. Gerald, ed., *A Historical Guide to Edgar Allan Poe (Historical Guides to American Authors)*. New York: Oxford University Press, 2001.

Phillips, Mary E., *Edgar Allan Poe – The Man*. Vol. I, Chicago, Philadelphia [etc.]:The John C. Winston Co. 1926.

Poe, Edgar Allan, *Essays and Reviews*. New York: The Library of America, Viking Press, 1984

Poe, Edgar Allan, *The Portable Edgar Allan Poe*. ed. Philip Van Doren Stern, New York, London [etc]: Penguin Books, 1997.

Quinn, Arthur Hobson *Edgar Allan Poe*. Baltimore: Johns Hopkins University Press; Reprint edition (December 1, 1997).

Rosenheim, Shawn James *The Cryptographic Imagination: Secret Writing from Edgar Poe to the Internet*. Baltimore, Md. : Johns Hopkins University Press, 1997.

Silverman, Kenneth, *Edgar A Poe: Mournful and Never-ending Remembrance*. New York, NY : Harper Collins Publishers, 1991.

Thomas, Dwight and David K Jackson, *A Documentary Life of Edgar Allan Poe 1809-1841*. Boston: G. K. Hall and Co., , 1987

Thomas, Dwight, "James F. Otis and 'Autography': A New Poe Correspondent, "from *Poe Studies*, vol. VIII, no. 1, June 1975.

Walker, Ian M. *Edgar Allan Poe : The Critical Heritage (Critical Heritage)*. London; New York: Routledge; & K. Paul, 1986.

Whalen, Terence, *Edgar Allan Poe and the Masses*. Princeton, N.J: Princeton University Press, 1999.

Enotes: The Raven Summary at eNotes <http://www.enotes.com/raven/>

McGraw-Hill Primis Online: Library of the Future – Edgar Allan Poe <http://www.mhhe.com/primis/catalog/pcatalog/D10-1.htm?http://www.mhhe.com/primis/catalog/pcatalog/F2033843.htm>

The Edgar Allan Poe Society of Baltimore http://www.eapoe.org>

The Poe Archive <http://www.thepoearchive.0catch.com/>

On or related to other individuals

"Poems, by P. P. Cooke", *Southern Literary Messenger, devoted to every department of literature and the fine arts*. / Volume 13, Issue 7, July 1847, pp.437-441.

"Report of the proceedings on the occasion of the Reception of the Sons of Newburyport, Resident Abroad, July 4, 1854", *The Newburyport Celebration*. Newburyport, MA: Moses E. Sargent, 1854

"The Prompter. Cornelius Matthews.", *The Living Age* ... / Volume 26, Issue 325, August 10, 1850.

"Writings of Cornelius Mathews", *The Southern Quarterly Review*, Volume 6, Issue 12, Oct 1844. pp. 307-342.

Acts and Resolutions Passed at the First Session of the Twenty-Sixth Congress of the United States. Washington: S.D. Langtree, 1840.

Belford, Barbara, *Bram Stoker and the Man Who Was Dracula*. Cambridge, MA:Da Capo Press, 2002.

SOURCES

Bibliotheca dramatica. Catalogue of the theatrical and miscellaneous library of the late William E. Burton, the distinguished comedian, comprising an immense assemblage of books relating to the stage...To be sold at auction by J. Sabin & co. ... October 9. 1860. New York: J. Sabin and Co.,1860.

Brodie, Fawn McKay, *No Man Knows My History: The Life of Joseph Smith : The Mormon Prophet.* New York : A.A. Knopf, 1945.

Brown, Walter Lee, *A Life of Albert Pike.* Fayetteville: The University of Arkansas Press, 1997.

Cole, Phyllis, *Mary Moody Emerson and the Origins of Transcendentalism: A Family History.* New York : Oxford University Press, 1998.

Cooke, Philip Pendleton, *Recollections of Philip Pendleton Cooke.* 1858.

Grenville Mellen, *A Book of the United States: exhibiting its geography, divisions, constitution and government ... and presenting a view of the republic generally, and of the individual states; together with a condensed history of the land, from its first discovery to the present time. The biography ... of the leading men; a description of the principal cities and towns; with statistical tables.* New York: H.F. Sumner & Co., 1840

Griswold, Rufus Wilmot, *The Poets and Poetry of America.* New York: James Miller, Publisher, 1872.

Habegger, Alfred, *My Wars Are Laid Away in Books* : The Life of Emily Dickinson. New York : Random House, 2001

Higginson, Thomas Wentworth, "Lydia Maria Child", *Contemporaries, vol 2, Writings of Thomas Wentworth Higginson.* Cambridge:The Riverside Press, 1900.

London, Jack, *The Portable Jack London (Viking Portable Library).* ed. Earle Labor, New York, London [etc]: Penguin Books, 1994

Parker, Hershel, *Herman Melville: A Biography : 1819-1851.* Vol. 1, 1819-1851., Baltimore : Johns Hopkins University Press, 1996.

Paulding, Hiram, *Journal of a cruise of the United States schooner Dolphin among the islands of the Pacific Ocean and a visit to the Mulgrave Islands, in pursuit of the mutineers of the whale ship Globe.* Australia and New Zealand Book Co, 1970.

Reynolds, David S., *Walt Whitman's America.* New York: Knopf, 1995

Sketches and Eccentricities of Col. David Crockett of West Tennessee. New York: Arno Press, 1974.

Thomas, F. W., *Sketches Of Character And Tales Founded On Fact.* Louisville, KY: Randolph, Wirt, Kenton, &c., 1849

Tuckerman, H. T., *The Life of John Pendleton Kennedy.* New York : G.P. Putnam & sons, 1871

Afrigeneas:Afrigeneas Library:Blacks Residing in Baltimore:Colored Householders Baltimore City Directory 1845 <http://www.afrigeneas.com/library/baltimore/1845%5Ba-l%5D.html>

American University:Music Sung and Played on the Fourth of July in the Nineteenth Century <http://www.american.edu/heintze/songs.htm>

AppLit – Resources for Readers of Appalachian Literature: Davy Crockett and Sally Ann Thunder Ann Whirlwind Crockett <http://www.ferrum.edu/applit/bibs/tales/crockett.htm>

Bedford/St.Martin's:LitLinks:Fiction - Catherine Maria Sedgwick (1789-1867) <http://www.bedfordstmartins.com/litlinks/fiction/sedgwick.htm>

Biographical Directory of the United States Congress:EVERETT, Edward, (1794 - 1865) <http://bioguide.congress.gov/scripts/biodisplay.pl?index=E000264>

Catharine Maria Sedgwick <http://www.geocities.com/delilah024/eng323CMSedgwick.html>

Compedit – Studies in American Humor: "*COL. CROCKETT'S EXPLOITS AND ADVENTURES IN TEXAS:* DEATH AND TRANSFIGURATION" <http://www.compedit.com/crockett.htm>

Gallery of History: Document 24337 HIRAM PAULDING <http://www.galleryofhistory.com/archive/9_2001/military/ADMIRAL_HIRAM_PAULDING.htm>

Goddesschess Partnership - Alpheta's Poetry Agora <http://www.goddesschess.com/poetryagora/turk.html>

Juvelis Books:Catalogue 25 Fall Miscellany - 54. Gould, Hannah F[lagg]. Gathered Leaves: or Miscellaneous Papers. Boston: William J. Reynolds, 1846. <http://www.juvelisbooks.com/catalog25-31%20thru%2060.html>

Lexicorp.com:The Atheneum - PALFREY, John Gorham. American Unitarian clergyman and historian. AUTOGRAPH LETTER SIGNED (1835) <http://www.lexicorps.com/Stock.htm>

MORMONISM:The Anthon Affair <http://www.foxgrape.com/anthon.htm>

New Advent:Catholic Encyclopedia: Orestes Augustus Brownson <http://www.newadvent.org/cathen/03001a.htm>

Old and Sold Antiques Auction and Marketplace: Some Avenue Clubs In The Early Days
    <http://www.oldandsold.com/articles08/fifth-avenue-7.shtml>
Pacific County Historical Society and Museum:The Sou'wester - Volume XXXVII, Special Annual
    Edition for 2002 <http://www.pacificcohistory.org/sw2002_1.htm>
Public Domain Music:American Composers - "When Thou Wer't True"(1843) Words by F. W.
    Thomas, Esq.Music by John Hill Hewitt, 1801-1890
    <http://www.pdmusic.org/hewitt/jhh43wtwt.txt>
Sonnet Central - Epes Sargent (1830-1880) <http://www.sonnets.org/sargent.htm>
The Life and Works of Herman Melville: The Origin of the Name "Moby
    Dick"<http://www.melville.org/mobyname.htm>
The New Jersey Historical Society: Archives-Manuscript Group 785, Kinney Family (Newark, NJ)
    <http://www.jerseyhistory.org/findingaid.php?aid=0785>
The Rettinger Home Page:Byrd.GED <http://www.larrett.com/rettinger/GED/Byrd.GED>
University of Chicago: American Poetry Full-Text Database – Bibliography
    <http://www.lib.uchicago.edu/efts/AmPo1/AmPo.bib.html>
University of Chicago:The Voltaire Society of America - Catherine Maria Sedgwick, 1839
    <http://humanities.uchicago.edu/homes/VSA/Sedgwick.html>
University of South Carolina :The Samuel D. Langtree American Pamphlets Collection
    <http://www.sc.edu/library/spcoll/hist/sdl.html>

Reference

*A Dictionary of American Authors deceased before 1950.*Compiled by Wallace, W. Stewart, Toronto:
    The Ryerson Press, 1951.
Duyckinck, Evert A. & George L, eds., *Cyclopaedia of American Literature.* 2 vols. Philadelphia:
William Rutter & Co., 1880.
Kunitz, Stanley J. And Howard Haycraft Wilson, eds., *American Authors 1600-1900.* New York: The
    H. W. Wilson Company, 1930.
Merriam-Webster's Dictionary of American Writers. Springfield, MA: Merriam-Webster Incorporated,
    2001.
Thomas, J. *Universal Pronouncing Dictionary of Biography and Mythology.* Philadelphia: J. B.
    Lippincott and Co. 1871.
Wilson, James Grant and John Fiske, eds., *Appleton's Cyclopedia of American Biography.* 6 vols,
    New York: D. Appleton and Company, 1887-1889.

About:Women's History < http://womenshistory.about.com/>
Bartleby.com:Bartlett's Quotations-Alphabetic Index of Authors
    <http://www.bartleby.com/100/a0.html>
Canadian Poetry:Poems In Early Canadian Newspapers:Author Index
    <http://www.uwo.ca/english/canadianpoetry/newspaper/author_index.htm>
Sperling, Joy, "'Art, Cheap and Good:' The Art Union in England and the United States, 1840–60",
    Nineteenth Century Art Worldwide, Volume 1, Issue 1, Spring 2002. <http://www.19thc-
    artworldwide.org/spring_02/articles/sper.html>
Strangers To Us All – Lawyers and Poetry <http://www.wvu.edu/~lawfac/jelkins/lp-
    2001/intro/lp1.html>
Tales of the Early Republic - Sources used in *Tales of the Early Republic* – Periodicals
    <http://www.earlyrepublic.net/bb/pk.htm>
Tales of the Early Republic:Brief Biographies from the Jackson/Van Buren Era (I)
    <http://www.earlyrepublic.net/BIOG-I.htm>
The Library of Congress: American Memory <http://memory.loc.gov>
University of Michigan: Making of America <http://www.hti.umich.edu/m/moagrp/>
University of North Carolina at Chapel Hill: Documenting the American South
    <http://docsouth.unc.edu/index.html>
University of Virginia: Early American Fiction Collection
    <http://etext.lib.virginia.edu/eaf/pubindex.html>
Women Writers: Domestic Goddess <http://womenwriters.net/domesticgoddess>

SOURCES

General

Anthony, Carl Sferrazza, *First ladies: the saga of the presidents' wives and their power.* Vol. I , New York: W. Morrow, 1990-1991.

Baym, Nina, *Woman's Fiction: A Guide to Novels by and About Women in America, 1820-70.* University of Illinois Press, 1993.

Bellesiles, Michael A., *Arming America: The Origins of a National Gun Culture*, Soft Skull Press, 2003.

Bercovitch, Sacvan, ed., *The Cambridge History of American Literature: Volume 2, Prose Writing 1820-1865 (The Cambridge History of American Literature).* Cambridge [England] ; New York :Cambridge University Press, 1995.

Brooks, Stephen, *America Through Foreign Eyes: Classic Interpretations of American Political Life.* Canada: Oxford University Press, 2002.

Grey, Robin, *The Complicity of Imagination : The American Renaissance, Contests of Authority, and Seventeenth-Century English Culture (Cambridge Studies in American Literature and Culture).* Cambridge ; New York : Cambridge University Press, 1997

Hertzberg, Arthur, *The Jews in America : four centuries of an uneasy encounter : a history.* New York : Simon and Schuster, 1989.

Hume, John F. *The abolitionists Together with personal memories of the struggle for human rights 1830-1864.* New York and London: G. P. Putnam's sons, the Knickerbocker Press.

Jusdanis, Gregory, *The Necessary Nation.* Princeton: Princeton University Press, 2001.

Lebow, Eileen F., *The Bright Boys : A History of Townsend Harris High School (Contributions to the Study of Education).* Westport, Conn.: Greenwood Press, 2000.

Lehuu, Isabelle, *Carnival on the Page: Popular Print Media in Antebellum America.* Chapel Hill, N.C. : University of North Carolina Press, 2000.

McCaughey, Robert A. *Stand, Columbia: A History of Columbia University in the City of New York, 1754-2004.* New York: Columbia University Press, 2003.

McCutcheon, Marc, *Everyday Life in the 1800s: A Guide for Writers, Students & Historians (Writer's Guides to Everyday Life).* Cincinnatti, OH: Writer's Digest Books, 1993.

Myers, Gustavus, *History Of The Great American Fortunes.* New York: The Modern Library, 1936.

Purchase, Eric, *Out of Nowhere: Disaster and Tourism in the White Mountains.* Baltimore, London: Johns Hopkins University Press, 1999.